The Beijing Opera Murder
An Inspector Bao Zheng Mystery

CHRIS WEST

© Chris West 1994.

Chris West has asserted his rights under the Copyright, Design and Patents Act, 1988, to be identified as the author of this work.

First published as *Death of a Blue Lantern* by Collins Crime in 1994.

This edition published in 2020 by Sharpe Books.

For Mandy.

CONTENTS

Chapters 1 – 18

The Dragon slept, tortured by its dreams.
But then it began to stir…

When the Queen sang, her voice soared up then plummeted down like the roller coaster in the Cultural Park. When she spoke, she fired out whole groups of syllables like a machine-gun then took one and teased the audience with it. The General nodded his head, sending long ripples up the pheasant feathers of his headdress. Gongs and clappers rang out as two men with wooden swords thumped onto the stage and began slashing violently at one another.

Detective Inspector (Second Class) Bao Zheng of the Beijing *Xing Zhen Ke* (Criminal Investigation Department) made his way up the aisle and squeezed onto the end of one of the long wooden benches that made up the seats of the opera house. Late again!

Bao only came here once a month, but work always seemed to interfere. Last time he'd had to type up some report. This time the team was back from Huashan and there had been a pointless, meandering discussion about the thefts. This thought made him angry, and he lit a cigarette to calm himself.

It was Panda brand, for Party members only. Almost everyone else in the opera audience – mainly old men with close-cropped hair, work-wrinkled faces and gap-toothed grins – would be rotting their throats with stuff like Flying Horse. Bao inhaled deeply and reminded himself of his good fortune.

The on-stage action subsided. The young hero began to sing, accompanied only by the *erhu*, a two-stringed violin that had been played in Bao's home province of Shandong for thousands of years. The old General was a fool: only the young Prince could rescue the state from its overwhelmingly superior opponents, and do so by cunning. Use the enemy's strength against them…

Everyone in this place was fortunate, Bao thought, to know and love *jingju*, Beijing Opera, to share and be elevated by the culture from which it came.

Bao took the last, best drag on the Panda and stubbed it out on the floor. Recently a Party directive had advised members to cut down on smoking for health reasons. But what did Cao Cao, the great soldier-poet, say?

'Drink and sing! How long is life?'

*

The players stood on the stage applauding the audience. The audience responded by stampeding for the doors. This was not out of disrespect but from necessity. Last buses ran early; those that had come by bike might have long rides home. Many of them would be required back on factory floors at six o'clock next morning. Bao Zheng, with a flat near Temple of Heaven Park and a desk that he did not need to be manning till half past seven, could take his time, relax and let the piece replay itself in his mind. The Queen had been particularly good, he thought, showing a full range of emotions, not just in the more obvious, attention-grabbing, high-pitched passages… Only when the hall was empty – apart from a drunk who had fallen asleep in the back row and two cleaners swishing brooms by the front exit – did he get up and walk slowly out into Dazhalan, the alley outside.

The street was busy with shoppers. A few years ago, most would have been in blue denim Mao suits. Now, many people, especially the young, had taken to Western-style jackets and shirts with wide lapels (still in sober colours, even for women's blouses). The Chairman was still present: a stall was selling T-shirts with his face on, for Western tourists. During Bao's youth this would have been sacrilege. Now, in 1991, it was good business. Western music blared from a shop. People seemed to be listening to more and more of this horrible stuff. More to Bao's taste was the crisp, clean smell of dough-sticks being deep-fried on a trolley by a young Mongolian. He reached into his pocket for a two-*jiao* note.

The image wouldn't go away. There had been something strange about that sleeping figure in the last row; something that he, as a policeman, had to investigate. He looked at the queue for the dough-sticks, shook his head and began pushing his way back to the theatre.

By the time he arrived, the sweepers had built two mountains of rubbish and were working hard on a third. The figure was still leaning against the rear wall, his head at the same slight angle, his hands still by his side, his complexion still as white as the dough on the stick-maker's stand.

'Are you all right?' Bao called out.

No reply. He made his way up the row and shook the man by the shoulders. The head moved stiffly. He took his plastic-covered police ID and held it up to the fellow's mouth. Not a droplet of breath. He didn't even try resuscitation.

For a moment, he thought of phoning the authorities anonymously. He wanted to go home and sleep. Night staff got paid night rates; they could come and sort this out. But his sense of duty, that shadow companion of Cao Cao's drinking and singing, rebelled – as it always did.

One, check the body for foul play. Not that that was very likely, in such a public place. Two, search for –

Bao stopped, dumbfounded. At the back of the man's neck was a small hole surrounded by dry, black blood. This man had been coldly, expertly murdered, right here at the opera.

Chapter One

'It's a disgrace!' said Team-leader Chen, thumping his desk.
'I found the body,' Bao replied.
'So what?'
'That makes me uniquely placed to solve the crime.'
'You're part of a team. My team.' Chen gestured round the grey-walled office at the other policemen present: Inspector (First Class) Zhao, Sergeant Fang, Constables Lu, Tang and Han. 'You can't just walk off cases when you feel like it. In all my time in the force –'

'These are my orders,' Bao cut in quickly. 'To investigate this killing. Starting today.'

The team-leader gestured at the pile of papers in front of him. 'The Huashan operation is of great importance. Your role in it is essential.'

Bao grinned to hide his embarrassment. His role was 'coordinator', a grand title which actually meant he stayed at HQ checking background information and answering a phone. This phone was reasonably busy, now that there was a reward for information leading to a successful conviction of the Huashan thief, but the quality of information had so far been very poor. Meanwhile, the real detective work was going on at the site, an archaeological dig sixty miles north west of the capital, from which a number of artefacts had disappeared. Bao hadn't even been there. His 'essential' role required little intelligence and even less initiative.

It was the sort of job he'd been getting for the last couple of years. Due to his age, he kept telling himself. Now he'd hit forty, it was younger, better connected men (and the occasional woman) on fast-track promotion schemes who were getting the interesting work.

'Thank you, Comrade Chen,' he said cautiously. 'But given the steady progress being made by the team, I feel I can safely delegate my work here to one of our junior team members. It will be good experience for them.'

Chen nodded. 'Steady progress. Yes, I believe that sums up the situation well.'

'I'll be working from here, too. So I can be called upon if absolutely necessary.'

Chen nodded again, then picked up a sheet of paper. 'It says here I'm to second a junior to you from our team.'

Bao stayed silent. Chen couldn't object. Orders were orders.

The team-leader took off his glasses and gave them a clean, something he often did when embarrassed. 'Take Lu,' he said finally. The two other constables, older more experienced men, showed no emotion, though Bao guessed they would be amused.

'I shall insist that you are both back on my case within a fortnight,' Chen went on.

Bao nodded assent. Team-leader Chen had lost enough face already. If the murder were a relatively simple affair, he should have it cleared up in that time. If not, then he could make a direct appeal to the Unit Party Secretary, 'Hawk' Wei. Not something he relished, but if it were necessary ...

Bao retired to his own office, where he took his pile of Huashan papers, carried them across to a corner and dumped them there. As he turned to face an empty desk he felt a rush of excitement. A case of his own again!

*

The two men stood in the mortuary, Bao in his neatly pressed olive-green police uniform with bright gold and blue epaulettes and yellow ribands, Dr Zhang in a grey overall smeared with blood. Beside them, the victim lay under a plastic sheet.

'The weapon was a small, sharp knife,' said Zhang. 'The killer knew what he was doing. One insertion, severing the medulla. Death was almost instantaneous. No shouts or screams, and very little blood.'

'Much force needed?'

Zhang shook his head. 'No. Just skill.'

'Any information from the nature of the wound?'

'Not much. The killer was sitting on the victim's left, obviously. Probably about average height, right-handed and reasonably strong. But this is about finesse, not force.'

Bao nodded. 'Time of death?'

'Around seven-thirty.'

'Not later?'

'I don't think so. We can't be a hundred per cent accurate.'

Bao had guessed as much – rigor mortis takes at least an hour to set in – but would like to have been proven wrong. 'So he must have sat there, dead, through most of the performance.'

'That's one piece of good fortune for him,' said Zhang jokily: not everybody liked traditional opera.

Bao ignored the comment. 'It's dark in those back seats. It's noisy during fight scenes. I suppose that's a better place to kill someone than the open street. But it's still a very strange place for a murder.'

'Do we have a name for him yet?'

The victim had not been carrying any ID, only a dirty handkerchief and a Martial Arts magazine.

'I'm afraid not. We've taken fingerprints, but the computers have encountered unexpected problems.'

'Why am I surprised to hear that?' said Bao. The correct attitude to technology was to welcome it unreservedly. But Bao couldn't bring himself to trust it. Computers, the new switchboard system, the new radios they had recently been issued with – all 'encountered unexpected problems'. Patience was expected. Why?

Maybe that was his age again. *Aiya,* couldn't we stay young forever?

The inspector pulled back the cover and stared at the corpse's scarred, moustachioed face. Late twenties. Good-looking, Bao reckoned, though he didn't really know what women liked. Not your standard operagoer, but so what? Beijing Opera was still a people's art-form. Anyone could attend; all sorts did.

But this one nameless, lifeless individual – why had he come? To meet someone? To escape from someone? Or was this a pointless, random killing, of the kind Bao read about happening in the West?

*

Constable Lu sat in the office, which was now otherwise empty, as the rest of the team had returned to Huashan. Most of the morning, he had been typing a report on a machine that built up characters stroke by stroke. He felt he was due a rest. His boss was next door, on the phone. Lu took out his latest mini-computer game, turned the sound off and began to play.

World Cup Football. Select two teams. China versus Brazil. Two sets of bandy-legged players began waddling across the little screen, passing a square ball to one another. Goal! China one, Brazil nil. Too easy – take it up a level. Damn! One all.

'Working hard, Lu?'

'*Aiya!* Yes, sir. Well, no, sir. I just started a minute ago, sir.'

Bao knew he should get angry, but there was something about Lu that reminded the inspector of himself at nineteen. Not the youngster's slow-wittedness nor his privileged background, but a simplicity of outlook, a lack of guile.

'Who was that on the line, sir?'

'Technical,' Bao replied. 'They've got us a name for our murder victim. Xun Yaochang. I want you to check the records here. I'll go and do his *hukou*.'

Lu grinned. *Hukou* records, the stuff of day-to-day surveillance kept at outlying police stations, were boring. Criminal files were a lot more exciting.

'I want a report by three-thirty.'

'Yes, sir.' The young man jumped to his feet and lolloped out into the corridor.

Bao went back to his office, lit a Panda, tilted his chair back and gazed round at the bulging metal filing-cabinets, the dusty wall-map of the capital, the narrow window, the grey stone floor and, right opposite him, his calligraphy scroll. This featured two characters in bold, free-flowing Zen style: *Zheng Yi*, justice. He had made them himself, in the correct manner, meditating in silence on their meaning then picking up a weasel-hair brush and dashing them down in an instant. He was proud of them. They were solid but infused with life, just as justice itself should be. His thoughts went back to Nanping Village, and his father, a peasant with a passion for education, giving him the characters to study. Along with the works of Marx, Lenin and Mao, Liu Shaoqi's *How to be a Good Communist*, and the classics of literature like *Journey to the West* and *The Romance of the Three Kingdoms*.

He exhaled and watched the smoke curl up towards the striplight. Was he being selfish, taking this case and letting his colleagues battle on with the seemingly insoluble business at Huashan? 'Bourgeois individualism,' his father would have called it, the sin of putting one's own desires above the general good. His eyes returned to the scroll. But what crime could be worse than the taking of life?

*

A group of 'little generals' – boys in oversize People's

Liberation Army caps and tunics that came down to their ankles – watched as the rider drew up outside Chongwen District Number Two Police Station and parked his motorbike under a torn canvas awning. The lads tried to guess the status of the new arrival, as Bao wore no badge of rank.

'He's just a sergeant,' said one. 'Look at that *Happiness* bike. If he were anyone senior, he'd have a Japanese one.'

'Perhaps he's in disguise,' said another. 'The head of the *Ke Ge Bo*, on a top-secret mission.'

'You shouldn't call it that,' said a third, whose father was a Model Worker. 'The Internal Security Bureau is essential to prevent sabotage and counter-revolutionary activity.'

The object of this discussion paused to look at the poster on the notice board by the station entrance, a cartoon account of a recently solved fraud case, whose last frame showed the criminal kneeling on the ground, blindfolded, about to be executed. Then he carried on up the steps.

'*Hukou* office is on the left,' the duty sergeant told him. 'Second door down.'

Bao found a young constable in shirtsleeves filling in forms by the light of a bare bulb. Precipices of paper rose up on all four walls. These were *hukou* files, on everyone who lived in Number Two area. They contained their work record, their family background, any reported anti-social behaviour, any close contact with outsiders and their visits (if any) to other parts of the country. There would be no exceptions, for without a *hukou* file nobody could get ration tickets for cooking oil, soap, clothing, noodles or rice.

'I want information on someone called Xun Yaochang,' said Bao. 'He was murdered last night.'

The constable showed no emotion, just checked the character Xun in a directory, crossed to the far corner and pulled out a file. Bao blew dust off it and sat in a corner reading.

Xun had come to Beijing five years ago, from somewhere in Hebei Province that Bao had never heard of. (Who was informing the victim's parents of the death? he wondered.) Many other young men from around China were now doing the same, heading for the cities in search of opportunity. Some were finding it. For Xun, things had not gone so well. He had an address in the worst part of the district, a patchy work record and a list of complaints by neighbours – drunkenness, playing loud music, repeated refusals to participate in voluntary campaigns. He had had 'dealings with the police', but these were not specified. Lu, no doubt, would find detail on these.

Bao wondered if Xun had arrived with the intention of living this life, or if he had come with better plans and slowly sunk into it.

'Did he sign for his ration tickets? he asked. 'I'd like to see his signature.'

'Signatures are at the back.'

Bao turned there.

'He's very irregular.'

'I'm afraid… we don't get signatures every week. We'd have queues going round the block if we did.'

Bao nodded. This was not correct procedure, but the station staff were no doubt overworked. It was not his place to criticize them.

Xun had signed his name in characters that were not the product of an illiterate or stupid man. The guy liked opera, Bao reflected. The bright kid who misses out somehow and turns to crime instead?

He made a note of Xun's address and that of the head of his Neighbourhood Committee, and handed the file back to the constable, who dropped it into a cardboard box.

'Dead people go downstairs,' said the constable

'I wonder if he will,' Bao replied, but the young man didn't get the joke.

*

Bao reckoned that the heads of Neighbourhood Committees fell into two categories. Some were kindly and experienced, giving their time freely to mediate in disputes, to care for the sick, and to advise youngsters heading in the wrong direction. Others seemed to do no good at all, were often nosey, petty and vindictive, and added to the unhappiness of the people they were supposed to serve.

'Good riddance,' said Mrs Wan when Bao told her of Xun's murder.

'He was a bad element?' he asked.

'Thoroughly. Alcohol, fighting, noise at night-time. Trouble with the police: I'm surprised you have to ask me about him.'

Bao was about to launch an explanation about how specific criminal records were stored at more central locations, but decided not to bother.

'Girls used to come and stay the night at his flat, too,' Mrs Wan went on. 'There's not room for two beds in there. I looked in through the window once and –'

'Different girls or always the same girl?'

'Different ones most of the time.'

Bao nodded. Xun must have been quite a charmer, then. He felt a shiver of disapproval – and behind that, though he hardly dared admit it, a touch of envy. Bao had not been good with women as a young man – his outgoing elder brother had surpassed him in that department (for all the good it had done him...) The great passion of his youth had – well, that was history.

'There was one who visited quite regularly until a few months ago,' Mrs Wan went on.

'D'you have her name?'

'No. Ask round Goldfish Alley.'

Bao nodded. Goldfish Alley was notorious for prostitution. 'But she hasn't been back recently?'

'No.'

'Can you describe her?'

'Overdressed. Men probably found her attractive, though she was too tall. I never spoke to her.'

Bao nodded. 'Tell me about Xun's work. "Businessman", it says in his *hukou*.'

Mrs Wan scowled. 'We all know what that means. Chairman Mao was right. All capitalists are black elements.'

'So you don't know what he actually did?'

'No idea.'

'Did he have any particular enemies?'

'Not that I know of.'

'So there's nobody who might have a reason to kill him?'

'Not that I can think of. But whoever did has done us all a favour.'

*

The old *hutong* alleyway where Xun had lived was typical of the area: narrow, winding, its surface cracked by tree-roots or subsidence. On either side rose windowless brick walls two or three metres high, many still topped with old glazed tiles, now chipped. Behind them would be old Qing Dynasty courtyards. These had once been the homes of rich officials and their retainers, but now they were mass housing and going to seed. Bao knocked at the thick wooden door of number 31.

No one answered. He knocked again. A young man in a T-shirt, jeans and reflector sunglasses appeared. 'What d'you want?'

'I'm looking for a fellow called Xun Yaochang,' said Bao, displaying his police ID.

'Don't know him.'

Bao narrowed his eyes. 'How long have you lived here?'

'I've got a residence permit.'

'I'm glad to hear it. Now answer my question. How long?'

'Couple of years.'

'So you must know Xun.'

'I see him about. What's he done?'

'He's dead.'

The young man seemed unmoved.

'Do you know anything about a woman he was seeing? A few months ago?'

'I kept out of his business.'

'Why?'

'I don't meddle in others' stuff and they don't meddle in mine.'

'You never saw any female with him?'

'No.'

Bao nodded. 'And you don't know anything about his business dealings?'

'No.'

'Any changes in his appearance in the last few months?'

'Dunno. Well – he looked smarter. Maybe he'd struck lucky somehow. No idea what or how, though. Sorry,' the young man added.

Bao gave him a smile for this tiny piece of politeness. 'Mind if I come in and look around?'

'I haven't got much choice, have I?' said the young man, reverting back to surliness.

Bao stepped over the stone lintel into the long, dog-leg hallway. A second door took him into the courtyard itself, a plot of bare earth about five metres square littered with rubbish, surrounded by single-storey accommodation. Bao knocked at a few doors, and got no reply.

'Which room was his?' he asked the young man, who had followed him into the quad.

'That one.'

Bao peered through the window. The room looked oddly empty.

'Has anyone been here and cleared it out?' he asked.

'Haven't seen anyone.'

He'd send a team to search it, anyway. Bao took a card out of his pocket. 'If you hear anything, can you give me a call? It might help us find out how this man died.'

'*Hao*,' said the young man. OK. He took the card and shoved it in a pocket without looking at it.

So many of the capital's young people were like this nowadays, Bao thought. Self-absorbed, surly, passionless. Would they really throw away everything the previous two generations had fought, sweated and died for? His mind went, as it often did, to events right at the heart of the capital, a couple of years previous.

*

Bao was back at HQ by three-thirty. Lu was ready with his report.

'Petty crime,' said the young man, clearly disappointed.

'Such as?'

'He is suspected of involvement in various rackets: currency dealing, unlicensed street trading, handling stolen goods.'

'Any convictions?'

'One for drunk and disorderly, one for stealing a bicycle …'

A recitation of minor offences followed. Bao listened, deep in thought, spinning a pen across the backs of his fingers like a propeller, a trick he'd learnt while recovering from the wounds he had received in Vietnam. Why kill such a petty operator? In a public place, therefore at some risk to the perpetrator?

'These rackets,' he said slowly. 'He works with others, I take it. Do we have any accomplices on record?'

'A few, sir. Someone called Wu Chengfa. Zhang Hua … There's a Meng Lipiao.'

The propeller stopped. 'Ah! Meng Lipiao will have a story for us! If we can find him.' Bao's voice faltered. He began staring at the dusty, pin-pricked map on the wall.

'Lu, have you ever wanted to own a nice piece of Ming Dynasty porcelain?'

'No, sir. I've always felt that antiquities are a common heritage and should belong to the People.'

'How about one made in Shanghai last week?'

'I thought the Ming Dynasty was a long time ago, sir.'

Bao paused. Was it worth explaining? No. He grabbed his jacket and made for the door, beckoning the rookie to follow.

Chapter Two

The clocks on the pagoda-topped towers of Beijing Main Station snapped round to the hour. Their chime began to boom out the opening bars of *The East is Red*. A few rustic faces lifted up to listen, but Beijingers had long since stopped taking notice of the old Maoist anthem. Bao checked his watch – it had started losing time recently – and began scanning the scene in front of him.

'Any sign of him, sir?' Lu asked.

'Not yet.'

The young man looked fretful.

'Patience, Lu,' Bao went on. '*Three feet of ice are not formed in one day.*'

The large open space in front of the station was, as usual, crammed. Soldiers stood in groups, the young recruits holding hands like children. Minorities from the mountains and deserts of the west sparkled in their bright clothes and flashing jewellery. Newly-prospering Han peasants from a million places like Nanping Village sat in family groups, stockaded behind bags full of the purchases that would give them so much face back home. *Lao bai xing*, old hundred names, the soil from which China's culture had grown over millennia.

Between these largely static islands of humanity moved the vendors and racketeers, selling food, magazines, soft drinks and black-market seat allocations, buying Hong Kong dollars or Foreign Exchange Certificates for grubby rolls of People's Money. In a far corner, a man had set up an illegal game of ace-in-the-hole. He was calling for bets; the fellow in his audience perpetually upping the stakes was obviously a plant but several travellers had been taken in. Another time, Bao would have done something about it. Today, he wasn't interested. None of the participants was Meng Lipiao.

'Let's wander about a bit more,' he told Lu.

They walked across the front of the station and into its vast marble main hall. THE PEOPLE'S RAILWAY SERVES THE PEOPLE, proclaimed a banner over the eighty-foot high map of China. An announcement about a late departure cut into the wistful folk music coming out of the tannoy. More waiting travellers, more vendors, no Meng.

The policemen moved back to the square then down a side alley full of tea-stalls and noodle cafes. There was a bristle of fear as they walked by. They reached the long-distance bus park.

'Ah!' Bao pointed to a man sitting on an irregular brick wall, surrounded by nick-nacks. 'There's our man.'

Lu began rolling up his sleeves.

'We're going to talk, Lu.'

The young man's face fell.

'If you want some action, go and wait by the Metro entrance. If he tries to run, that's the way he'll go. It'll be up to you to stop him. You've double-checked his recognition characteristics?'

'Of course,' Lu said, then did so. 'Dark glasses, leather jacket, jeans, height about one metre seventy.'

'Half the *liumang* in Beijing look like that, Lu. Find something special.'

'Er ...'

'That ridiculous haircut. The tear on the jacket sleeve. That fat leather belt – might be useful if you need to grab hold of him, too.'

Lu nodded.

'Now close your eyes. Bring his image to mind. Now open them again and double-check your image. Got him correctly?'

'Yes, sir.'

'Right. Metro entrance. Blend in. Have a story. Who are you waiting for?'

'This guy Meng, er – what's he called again?'

'A *story*, Lu. Think a story, and you'll look natural. Waiting for your girlfriend?'

'I haven't got a girlfriend.'

'Use your imagination. Now go.'

*

Meng Lipiao pointed to one of the objects on his tray. 'That's worth two hundred yuan,' he told the foreigner. 'At least. I can let you have it for one hundred and fifty.'

'Eighty?' said the foreigner.

'Eighty? This piece is two hundred years old. At least ... One hundred and forty. People's Money. In the shops –' Then Meng froze. '*Tamade!*'

The foreigner paused to look this word up in his phrase-book (it roughly means 'motherfucker', so he wouldn't have found it).

'Ten yuan. Take it!' Meng shouted.

The foreigner scratched his head and began reaching for his wallet – then saw what Meng had seen. A policeman heading his way. There was a tinkling sound as the pot hit the pavement.

'Hey!' Meng shouted as the foreigner fled in panic. He thought of doing the same, but Bao was too close.

'I've got a licence, officer.'

'I'm sure. For selling genuine goods at fair prices.'

'You heard me. Ten *kuai*, I was asking that ghost-devil.'

'Foreign friends, we call them nowadays.' Bao picked up a bowl with a blotchy red glaze and looked at the markings on the bottom. '*Xuande* reign? That must be worth a bit.'

Meng smiled. Bao threw the bowl on to the pavement.

'Even by your standards that's rubbish.' Bao picked up another bowl. 'Tang Dynasty? And it looks so new! Mind if I show it to a colleague in the fraud squad?'

Meng sighed. 'How much d'you want? The last gold-badge was happy with ten *kuai* a week.'

'I don't take bribes.'

'You're a policeman.'

'I want to talk.'

'What about?'

'An old colleague of yours. Xun Yaochang.'

Meng flinched. 'Who?'

'Your old colleague.'

'I haven't seen him for years.'

'Let's start back then, shall we?'

'OK,' said Meng.

Bao must have relaxed the tiniest bit. Suddenly there was a crash of tumbling crockery and the huckster was away into the crowd. The inspector, wrong-footed, was behind him. Too far behind.

'Stop that man!' he called out.

A group of boy soldiers watched gormlessly as Meng jinked past them.

'Stop that man!'

An old woman bravely reached out a hand but Meng swept her aside.

Then he was gone, swallowed up by the people.

*

Constable Lu leant against the wrought iron railings around the Metro entrance, staring at the passers-by. A young woman strutted past in a short skirt and black stockings. A southerner, no doubt. No morals, those southerners. A good Socialist does not waste thoughts on –

There was a commotion in the crowd ahead. Someone was barging towards him. Haircut, jacket – what was the third one?

Who cared? This was the guy. Lu moved towards him. Meng spotted him and turned back into the crowd. Lu gave chase. He was young and fit, and was soon gaining on his quarry. Meng turned into an alley. Lu followed. Meng realized the alley was blind. He stopped and turned to face his adversary. Lu stopped too. The two men stared at each other.

Bao Zheng had this saying about dogs and people in impossible situations. Lu couldn't remember it, but he knew its basic message: this guy could get nasty. For a second, the young man's courage failed and he took a step back – and Meng was running at him. Shamed by his momentary weakness, Lu crouched forward and spread his arms. Meng tried to swerve past but Lu grabbed him and pulled him to the ground, which he hit with a thud and a cry of pain. Lu had handcuffs on him in an instant.

A small crowd of people gathered.

'What's he done?' said one.

'Criticized the government, probably,' said another.

*

'All we want is some help,' said Bao.

'You've a bloody strange way of asking for it.'

'You've an even stranger way of offering it.'

Silence fell. 'Why me?'

'You were a colleague of his. Pretty close, by all accounts.'

'I was. I'm not any longer.'

'Why not?'

'No reason. We're just – not.'

'You two once had a nice racket in stolen goods. What happened to it?'

'It stopped.'

'Why?'

'Because it did.'

'D'you want the proper interrogators in?' said Bao, suddenly angry. 'It could easily be arranged.'

Meng glanced round at the room. Public Security HQ, Qianmen East Street. People could come in here and never reappear. He shook his head. 'Xun tried to cheat me.'

'When?'

'About six months ago.'

'Interesting. Tell us the story.'

Meng glanced around again.

'There aren't any bugs here,' Bao went on. 'Lu, put that pencil down. This is unofficial.'

The constable looked surprised but did as he was told. Meng began to speak.

'Xun had a camcorder – a lovely one, a Sony, still in its box. Of course, I've no idea where he got it from. I found him a client. We arranged to meet on a bus – one of those ones heading out into the suburbs. They're pretty empty midday.'

'Which bus?'

'A 352,' Xun answered without hesitation.

'Good. Carry on.'

'The client and I sat at the back. Xun was to get on a few stops from the end. If all was clear, we'd do a swap there and then. If there were too many other passengers, we'd go to a park near the last stop and do the swap there. But when Xun got on, he had three other guys with him.'

Meng shook his head, then continued. 'He told us to go to the park. So we did. Then he pulled a knife on us, took the camcorder, my client's wallet, even our shoes. Bastard!'

Bao nodded. 'And you haven't seen him since?'

'No.'

'You must be keen to get your own back.'

'You know the phrase, officer. *The past is like smoke.*'

'It gets everywhere and can poison people. Who were these three guys?'

'I don't know. Just toughs. The sort who prey on hard-working businessmen.'

'You seem particularly scared of these ones. Would you like to tell me why?'

'I'm not scared!'

Bao nodded, then turned to Lu and asked him to go and make tea for everyone.

'Including him?' Lu asked.

Bao gestured at Meng, who gave a nod.

'Tea for three,' said Bao. The young constable left the room.

'I mean what I say about our conversation being unofficial,' Bao went on, once he and Meng were alone. 'But I've also got a job to do. I could make things difficult for you if you leave me no choice. Tell me who those men were.'

Meng began twisting on his seat. Bao watched him in silence. Finally, the detective spoke. 'Why don't I tell you what I think was going on, and you can correct me?'

Meng seemed overcome with relief.

'Your friend Xun got bored with pulling small jobs like camcorders and decided to move up in the world. The people on the bus were his new colleagues. This was a test of loyalty. Ditch an old friend for us. I imagine you got a visit from them a few days later, telling you to keep quiet. How am I doing?'

Meng's relief had drained away. 'That's not ...' he began, but there was no conviction in his voice.

'I want the name of the gang and the names of any individuals you knew. Then you can go. None of this will ever be on the record.' He paused. 'Of course, if you don't tell me, we could keep you here for a very long time.' He sat back and let silence get to work again.

'Do you offer ... informant protection?' Meng said finally.

'Officially, no. Unofficially we'll keep a watch out for you. But right now nobody knows you've spoken to me, and I'm not telling anyone, so it shouldn't be necessary.'

Meng did not look convinced. 'How can I trust you?'

'Have I ever broken my word in the past?' said Bao. 'I know, I'm not out on the streets any longer. They keep me behind a desk. But it hasn't totally destroyed my sense of right and wrong. Or my need to keep my reputation good.'

Meng scowled.

'I need to get things sorted out before Xiao Lu gets back,' Bao went on. 'He's the son of a very senior Party official and does everything strictly by the rules.' He let the silence fall again. 'I'm feeling thirsty!' he exclaimed after a while. 'I'm so glad a nice mug of tea is on its way.'

Meng held out his hand and began tracing characters on it. Three of them. *Yi Guan Dao.*

Bao's eyes widened.

The petty criminal laughed. 'You think they're ancient history, don't you? The Party says the Triads have been – what's the word they use? Suppressed. Don't believe it.'

'I shan't,' said Bao.

Lu was back with the tea.

*

Bao made his way down to the basement, where the *Xing Zhen Ke* library was based. He was hoping to find Chai there. Many years ago, when Bao first came to the capital, he and this man had worked on a case together and 'clicked'. One evening, they had drunk too much and sworn brotherhood. A year or so later, Chai had been shot in the back by a gang of drug smugglers. Bao had worked extra hard to get the culprit brought to justice, and after the verdict, had asked to carry out the execution himself. Permission had been granted.

An assistant was on duty.

'If you'd like to fill in this form, we can let you have three files to take away,' she told him. 'You are allowed to keep them for twenty-four hours, after which time you will have to get clearance from the fifth floor.'

There was a buzzing noise and Chai's electric wheelchair rolled into view.

'Bao Zheng!' The occupant held out a hand, and Bao shook it with suitable warmth. 'What can I do for you?'

'I want all the information you've got on the *Yi Guan Dao* Triad.'

'All of it?'

'As much as you can spare. And I want it for as long as I need it.'

Chai nodded. 'Miss Hu, give the inspector everything he asks for.'

The assistant opened her mouth to protest then went off.

'So what brings about your interest in the Triads?' Chai continued. 'I thought you were investigating art thefts. Are the *Yi Guan Dao* involved in those?'

'No. It's a murder. Committed under my nose. Well, behind my back. Of a small-time hood who we think joined up.'

'Chopped to bits with meat cleavers, was he?'

'No, stabbed. But there's a Triad link, so I need to follow it up.'

'Ah. A bit like that business with the forged banknotes…' The two old colleagues began reminiscing until Miss Hu appeared with two armfuls of files.

'Those look heavy,' said Bao. 'Allow me.'

She glared at him. 'I was runner-up in the all-China Police Athletics Association decathlon. I used to lift this weight fifty times a day. Where is your office?'

'Third floor.'

'Follow me, please.'

Up in the office, Miss Hu put the files on his desk, acknowledged the inspector's thanks with the slightest of nods and walked out. Bao grinned, embarrassed by his own mixed reactions of annoyance and admiration. Then he selected a file at random and began to read.

Investigations into the activities of the Yi Guan Dao *Triad, by Detective Inspector (First Class) Liu Qiang.*

He glanced up at the clock. Half-past four. He'd skim through the stuff now and get home on time for once.

Next time he looked up, it had gone seven.

Chapter Three

Bao closed the file and stared blankly at its drab grey cover. His head spun with the information that lay within it. His colleague Liu's findings supported Meng's story. A Triad lodge had been set up in the capital, led by a figure known only as the Shan Master. The most senior figure for whom he had any possible identity was the lodge Red Stick (Enforcer), a man named Ren Hui, a businessman with good connections. The lodge appeared to be expanding. According to rumour, a swearing-in ceremony for 'Blue Lanterns' (new recruits) had been held about six months ago.

Liu had described what the ritual would be like.

To join a Triad meant to change your life, to die and to be born again – hence the term 'Blue Lantern' (Bao still remembered the old custom of hanging such lanterns outside the homes of the dead). The initiation ceremony was designed to impress upon the youngsters the totality of their new commitment. Bao imagined the man he had seen in the mortuary going through it – Xun and probably four or five other young males, in grey, kneeling to receive burning incense sticks from the Shan Master, which they would then dash to the floor to simulate their fate if they broke the Triad code. Next, they would swear the thirty-six Oaths of Loyalty. Each would prick their middle finger and let the blood ooze into a cup, from which they all drank (still, Bao wondered, now this Western disease called AIDS was beginning to infect China?) The Incense Master, the lodge's expert on ritual, would teach them the society's codewords and recognition signals, then the Shan Master would invite them to step across a symbolic river of burning paper – a one-way journey, according to Oath Thirteen.

Finally, they would take meat cleavers to an effigy of Ma Ningyi, the renegade monk who had betrayed the first Triad group, a reminder of the price of disloyalty.

Bao locked up his office and made his way down the stone steps of HQ into the main hall. The retired Special Forces sergeant on the front door wished him good night. Bao walked out into the smart concrete courtyard, then round to the rack at the rear of the building where his black Phoenix bicycle stood waiting for him. The motorbike he rode during work hours was a departmental one; only when he was Detective Inspector First Class would he have one that he could ride home. As he nosed the Phoenix out into the busy, jangling bike-lane of Qianmen East Street, he pondered what his next move should be. The author of that report, Liu – he must speak to him tomorrow morning.

A traffic light went red, and Bao pulled up. He wondered what Chen, Zhao and the rest of the team were doing now, back at Huashan.

Nothing remotely as interesting as this, he thought. He felt a big smile cross his face.

*

Bao put a call through first thing next morning.

'Can I speak to Inspector Liu Qiang?'

'No.'

'Why not?'

'He's dead.'

'Dead?'

'Heart attack, three months ago.'

Bao's eyes widened. 'Are you busy?'

'We're always busy.'

'I'm coming over now.'

*

Liu Qiang's colleagues remembered him with little affection.

'He was a loner,' said his team leader. 'An obsessive. I let him get on with his stuff as much as I could. He was very bitter about lack of support for his ideas.' The man gave a shrug. 'There was never enough money for the kind of investigation he wanted. He should have been born twenty years earlier. You know what it's like now, everything has to be costed.'

Bao nodded.

'He didn't keep fit,' the team leader went on. 'And he smoked. You've read the latest Party directive on smoking, of course?'

'Of course. Where did he die?'

'Here. He often used to work over lunch break. He lived for his job. One day, I came back and found him slumped over his desk.'

'Any clues as to – '

'It was natural. We had a post-mortem, but there were no signs of any foul play. Most of us wondered why it hadn't happened earlier.'

'So it was common knowledge, his heart condition?'

'Oh, yes. You'd only need to pass the poor old sod wheezing up the stairs. *The day is waning and the road ending.*'

Bao gave another nod. 'Does he have any family?'

'No.'

'None?'

'Not to our knowledge.'

Bao grimaced. Back in Nanping Village, life was still dominated by family and clan. Come to the capital…

'I guess we do feel guilty we weren't more friendly,' the team leader said suddenly. 'But he wasn't the sociable type. We'd all go out for a meal sometimes. Eat a bit, drink a bit. He never came with us.'

'Did he leave anything else apart from his Triad file?'

The team leader shook his head, but a sergeant began rummaging in a drawer.

'His diary,' he said, holding out a small green book.

Liu Qiang's name was in the front, in correct, careful calligraphy. Then came a few appointments and a work schedule. January was to be dedicated to the *Yi Guan Dao*. A name was written at the top of one page: Luo Pang. From February onwards, there was nothing.

'When did Liu die?' Bao asked.

'12 January.'

Bao returned to his own office, where he checked through Liu's file for references to Luo Pang. There were none. So was this a new suspect? The Shan Master, perhaps? Or just another password? Or a false trail? For the moment there didn't seem to be any way of finding out.

The inspector took a small black notebook out of his pocket, and began to write.

He had his own approach to cases, which he had worked out over the years. First, note down all actual facts about the case so far, however irrelevant they may seem. Then check they really are facts. What is actually known and what is presumed? Then consider what he called 'pressure points' – things that don't add up, people whose role in the story seemed false in some way – and what action should be applied there.

'The method' he called it. It wasn't infallible – nothing was, not even the Party – but it always helped.

*

Commissioner Da was seventy-five – almost old enough for the Politburo, as Bao's colleague Zhao said when Team-leader Chen wasn't around. Da had been on the Long March. He had fought the Japanese in Shanxi province, the Nationalists in Manchuria and the West in Korea. He had been fiercely criticized in the Cultural Revolution, then rehabilitated, rumour had it on the insistence of Premier Zhou Enlai himself. Now he sat in an office on the fifth floor where he appeared to spend all day drinking premium export-only tea and writing memoranda.

Bao Zheng, from a poor family in rural Shandong, would seem to have little connection to this darkly eminent, urbane man. But there was a link: the military. Bao had left Shandong at sixteen to join the People's Liberation Army, and had won a Combat Hero medal during China's invasion of Vietnam in 1979. After leaving the Army for the police, he had kept in touch with his old commanding officer on the Yunnan front. When Bao was posted to the capital, Colonel Li had told him to contact Da. Bao had done so, and the two men had taken a liking to one another.

Da respected Bao for his medal and for what he called his 'outlook'. They shared an interest in traditional Chinese culture. And Bao was a good listener to the old man's stories. Bao, in turn, genuinely enjoyed hearing the stories: his father had always advised him never to cultivate a relationship, however advantageous, if he did not feel genuine affection for the other person. He did not overuse the connection, either, sticking to professional, not personal favours.

'Ren Hui is our only way forward,' Bao explained. 'I must have a close look at him.'

Da took the lid off his tea-cup and sniffed the steam. 'Another minute, I think. Why don't you just pull him in for questioning?'

'It's too early. I want to get to know him a bit first.'

Da nodded. 'You know Internal Security aren't keen on *Xing Zhen Ke* personnel in plain clothes. They'll make a fuss.' The old man paused. 'But I'll get everything signed off. I don't like the way they meddle in our affairs.' He sniffed the tea again.

They ... On the floors below, people said that Commissioner Da (nobody called him the pally-sounding Lao Da, Old Da) worked for Internal Security. Da always denied it vigorously, but told Bao not to pass the denials on to anyone. 'If they dislike me enough to say that,' he would argue, 'it's best if they are also a little afraid of me.'

The old campaigner raised the mug to his lips took a sip. 'It is ready!'

Bao Zheng removed the lid of his own cup and began to drink, too. Da was right, of course. The taste was teetering on the edge of bitterness but not falling over it. Perfect!

*

A bloodshot sun was sinking behind the gables, smokestacks, trees, power-lines, apartment blocks and TV aerials that made the skyline of Chongwen, in 1991 the poorest of the capital's four inner districts. The air was heavy with smoke, heat and rush-hour racket – bicycle-bells, crowds jostling along the bumpy concrete pavements, and now, more and more, motor vehicles, which were demanding more and more space (if this growth went on, they'd outnumber the bicycles one day...) Somewhere, a traffic policeman blew a whistle. At whom? Nobody here knew; nobody here cared.

The taxi turned off the arterial road and was instantly back in the closed world of the *hutongs*. One of its passengers was Bao Zheng, now in a Western suit, patted the briefcase on his knee.

'Remember your name,' he told the other passenger, Lu.

'Yes, sir. It's Bo.'

'Just down here, isn't it, sir?' said the driver.

'That's right.' Bao glanced across at Lu again. Was his assistant the right companion for this mission? Lu would be good in a fight, but the best undercover operatives never got into fights in the first place. But Bao needed company. Two pairs of eyes were very much better than one. He was lucky to have an assistant at all.

The taxi pulled up by a clean, well-kept doorway and the two passengers got out. Bao watched the vehicle disappear, then walked up to the door and rang a bell.

A man soon appeared and showed the new arrivals in. They walked down a corridor, through an arch and into a well-kept yard. At the far end was a two-storey house with a facade of fresh stucco. Blinds on all its windows, except one in a kind of side annexe, kept out prying eyes. Somewhere inside it, a woman was singing a wistful folk tune.

'How lovely,' Bao muttered.

'What?' said Lu.

'The song.'

'Oh, yes.'

The man crossed to the stuccoed house and rapped four times on the door (Bao made a mental note of the rhythm). The door opened to reveal a stocky character in a pinstripe suit, black and white leather brogues and a bright purple shirt with matching tie. This had to be Ren Hui, importer/exporter, probably Enforcer for the local *Yi Guan Dao* lodge and possibly the killer of Xun Yaochang.

'Mr Ling! Come in,' said Ren, dismissing the gatekeeper with a flick of his hand.

The hall had thick pile carpet and what looked like silk wallpaper. Ren closed the door and bolted it, top and bottom.

'So you knew my old friend Shi?'

'That's right,' said Bao. 'Back in Jinan days, of course. Times have changed a lot since then.' He held out his card.

Ling Wuda. Procurement Manager, Victory Electronics Factory.

'Shi and I went in, er, different directions,' Bao continued. How thorough chain-smoking, Triad-obsessed Inspector Liu had been! 'But we've both moved on in the world.'

Ren laughed. 'And now you're after air-conditioners, right?'

'Yes. Productivity will tumble when summer comes. You know what it's like.'

'Not really.' Ren flicked a switch and a jet of cold air swirled past Bao's head. 'Come through.'

A huge television dominated one corner of the next room. Xinjiang carpets overlapped one another on the floor, and the walls were hung with tapestries.

'Drink, gentlemen?' Ren crossed to antique lacquer cupboard and opened it. The inside had been gutted and turned into storage space for bottles of foreign spirits. Bao reined in his disgust at such vandalism and asked for a beer. American, if possible.

Ren called out: 'Yujiao!' The singing stopped and a young woman entered from a side door. She was tall but graceful, with long hair tumbling over her shoulders, framing a face that Bao would have found beautiful had it not been made up to look vulgar and Western.

'These gentlemen want some American beer,' Ren said. 'Fetch us three, please.'

'Yes, Father.' She disappeared at once, then came back with three tins and glasses.

'My daughter is the best singer in the city,' said Ren.

Yujiao blushed but said nothing.

'And the most beautiful,' Ren continued.

She blushed even more.

Bao made a suitably polite comment, while an inner voice added that her beauty deserved more than this showing-off.

Having poured out the beers, the young woman headed for the door.

'Stay and amuse us, Yujiao,' Ren told her.

'I've work to do, *baba*.'

'Oh, very well.' After she'd gone, Ren shook his head. 'She knows her own mind, that girl. And she's so talented. Singing, dancing, acting. She's got a great future.' He raised his glass. '*Ganbei!*' Cheers!

'*Ganbei!*' the policemen replied, and drank. The singing began again, this time in a foreign language. Probably English, Bao thought, the language that everyone under thirty wanted to speak.

'Now, this machinery you want to get hold of. It's not easy to come by. I'll need an advance.'

'That won't be a problem. Would you prefer cash?'

'Of course.'

'How much?'

'Twenty per cent.'

Bao knew he had to play the part, so they haggled for a while and got the figure down to fourteen.

'I wish she'd sing something a bit more cheerful,' Ren said finally.

They talked some more about the deal. Before he became deskbound, Bao had used this alias several times in covert work, and it had not taken him long to update himself on developments in the air-con business. After a little more alcohol had been consumed, he steered the conversation onto business contacts, then dropped the name Xun Yaochang into it. Ren, who was halfway through a mouthful of beer, nearly choked.

'You've dealt with him?' he asked, wiping froth off his suit with a silk handkerchief.

'Only briefly. Was that unwise?'

'No. I don't really know the man. I've heard he's not very reliable, that's all. I wouldn't do business with him.'

'I won't,' said Bao. He didn't mention the name again; he didn't need to.

*

'So let's get him,' said Lu, as the two men sat in the back of another taxi.

Bao shook his head. 'We've found a link, but we've no real idea what it consists of.'

'Can't we just bring him in and work on him?'

Bao grimaced. He disliked the heavy-handed approach of some of his colleagues.

'This case isn't straightforward, Lu. If Xun simply broke the Triad code, he would have received "death by ten thousand swords" – or rather by five or six meat cleavers, wielded by Xun's fellow recruits under Ren Hui's supervision. Messy business. Instead he was killed, quite surgically, at an opera performance. Why?'

He looked thoughtful, then cheered up. 'But we have begun. Learn to savour moments like these, Xiao Lu. Detection is like jungle war. The enemy is out there. To start with you have no idea where. Then you get a clue: a sign, a story, something that leads you to where they might be. Sometimes that turns out to be false. But then the confirmations begin to build up. Then you spot a point of opportunity. Then you take that opportunity and win that battle. Then you follow it up, taking care not to be lured into any kind of trap. Finally, you make the decisive strike and victory is yours! We are still near the start but beginning to make progress.' He clapped the young man on the shoulder. 'Such times are good, Xiao Lu. Enjoy them!'

*

It was Friday. No work this afternoon; instead, Political Study. The team had returned from Huashan, in time to shower off the red dust that got over everyone who worked there and to smarten up for the session.

It was held in a lecture room with a stage and raised banks of seats. During the Cultural Revolution, this room had witnessed the humiliation of a number of the capital's finest police officers. Since then it had been the venue for regular Political

Study and the occasional talk on criminology. Party Secretary Wei took the chair, as usual.

'Today is a particularly important session,' Wei began, also as usual. 'Now, I know the incident on Tiananmen Square was nearly two years ago, but there are still, er, ramifications that have to be dealt with. Our leaders have decided to launch a new campaign, *Strengthen the Party*. I have details here.'

He glanced round at his audience. Usually people would have opened books or files by now and would be covertly reading them. But not after that announcement.

'It's quite simple. All Party members will make a thorough self-criticism of their thoughts and actions from 26 April to 4 June 1989. We will then formally resign our membership.' He paused, to let his words sink in. 'Then, of course, we apply to rejoin. The point is that vetting procedures, which we normally apply to others, will be applied to ourselves. All of us.' Wei grinned. 'This is not a trick. We have no quotas of rightists to fill. The aim is to increase our self-awareness, to see how we made mistakes, to prevent such mistakes happening again. I feel we should be glad of the opportunity the Party is offering us. A chance to close the door and think carefully. Honesty is the keyword. Comrade Bao, you don't agree?'

'Of course!' said Bao.

Why had Wei singled him out to ask?

*

Saturday night. Late. Bao was still at his desk. He made himself another cup of green tea, scratched his head, glanced up at his calligraphy scroll – JUSTICE – then returned his attention to the piece of paper in front of him.

My name is Bao Zheng. I am an Inspector (Second Class) in the Criminal Investigation Department of the Beijing Public Security Bureau. This is a detailed account of my thoughts and actions from 26 April to 5 June 1989.

Chapter Four

May 1989.

To start with, Bao Zheng had been hostile to the protesting students. They were a pampered elite messing up the life of the capital. They talked arrogantly to Party leaders. They were making China lose face in front of the whole world. He had volunteered for extra duty, to go out on to the streets and help the regular city police keep order. He'd been set to guard the census office, outside which a small group of protesters had encamped.

These youngsters seemed eager to talk with anyone. Bao, ever curious about people, found himself drawn into arguments.

'You should realize what the Party has achieved since liberation,' he told them, quoting the remarkable facts and figures – infant mortality, literacy rates, GNP levels – that all conscientious Party members have at their fingertips. 'In 1949 the life-expectancy of the average Chinese was below forty. Now it's seventy. What an achievement that is!'

'It's even higher in Taiwan,' said one of the students.

'It's higher still in Europe,' another chimed in.

A third, probably sensing the unwisdom of making these comparisons, said, 'We love our country. We want it to be as good as these places.'

'You must give the reforms time,' Bao replied.

'How much time?'

'We don't want to end our lives with China still backward,' said the young man.

'You won't. Why should you?'

'Because of corruption, nepotism, cover-ups of official incompetence. Only democracy will stop these things.'

Min zhu. Democracy. Bao found their parroting of this Western word annoying. Weren't they aware of all the things wrong with the West? But in other ways, he had to admit that the protestors had a point. There was corruption – as there always had been. Their intentions, he decided, were good. If only they'd tone down their objections and talk sensibly with their superiors. Harmony emerging from negotiation: that was the right way.

One day, a young woman came up to the inspector and offered him a flower. She had red cheeks, keen intelligent eyes and a gawky, peasant style of speech. Listening to her speak, Bao imagined himself in Nanping Village again. He saw its one, rutted street surrounded by narrow lanes and the Ancestral Hall, officially closed but still secretly decked with flowers, food and hell-money at Qing Ming or Autumn Moon. He saw the red brick Party offices where his father had sat struggling through paperwork. He took the gift, even though he knew he shouldn't.

Another evening, the protesters wanted to light a fire. That was also against the rules, but Bao let them go ahead, anyway. He was rewarded with real pleasure at the light glowing on their faces and the songs they sang. This brought back memories, too: of Army training, of camp in Yunnan, of the company of men and women prepared to fight and die for their country. When they began the *Internationale* he joined in quietly.

When summer came, they didn't need fires any longer. Tempers frayed in the rising heat. Troublemakers infiltrated their ranks – the types Bao later saw in official videos attacking Army vehicles with clubs and petrol bombs. He tried to warn 'his' students (he'd come to think of them that way) about these people. Their response was naïve. He wrote a memorandum to his superiors, advising them to distinguish carefully between genuine protesters and disruptive elements. Luckily for him, the document had got lost somewhere.

On 1 June, he was moved to Muxudi, a busy junction a couple of miles west of Tiananmen Square. The Army was closing in on the capital now, and a call had gone up for the townspeople to defend the students. Tens of thousands responded. Soldiers were sent in to disperse them; unarmed peasant recruits in trainers and casual clothes.

The Beijingers blocked the road and stood arguing with them. The recruits listened, then retreated in confusion. Bao watched them go with mixed feelings. Something had to be done to bring the capital back to normal. Making the People's Liberation Army look foolish was not that something. But what was?

Next evening the crowds were out again, and a new force was sent in, uniformed and armed. Bao recognized them at once as the Twenty-seventh Division from Shijiazhuang. These elite troops lined up and fired their AK47s into the air. The crowd began to disperse. Bao watched with approval. A nicely balanced show of force. Show them who's in charge, but nobody gets hurt.

Then the Kalashnikovs were lowered. An order was shouted, and the men began pumping bullets into the retreating Beijingers.

Bao couldn't believe it. The Army was firing on the People.

'Stop!' he found himself shouting. 'There must be a mistake! They have no weapons!'

Nobody heard. He began to run towards the soldiers.

'I demand to see your commanding officer!' he yelled, words that had sounded ridiculous then, let alone now. Then a bullet struck him in the leg and he fell to the ground. People were running all round him, screaming, in panic. Self-preservation took over and Bao began to hobble back with them. A nineteen-year-old girl pitched forward in front of him. He tried to pick her up, but the pressure of fleeing, terrified Beijingers drove him by. Glancing back, he saw blood pumping out of a great hole between her shoulders; there wouldn't have been any point in trying to help her, anyway. In a terrible second of absolute fury, he thought the unthinkable, that if he had a rifle of his own, he would turn round and use it against his own beloved People's Liberation Army.

Two days later, the same men went into Tiananmen Square. A clampdown followed. Bao, recovering from his injury, had had little to do with that. Now, two years on, things were returning to normal. But someone wanted them stirred up again.

'The gun shoots the bird that sticks its head up,' an inner voice whispered. It had a strong Shandong accent; it belonged to Laolao, his maternal randmother. 'Be patient. Yang gives way to Yin.'

Bao had kept his head down as an Army recruit during the Cultural Revolution and survived. He had kept his silence since June '89 and had survived. He'd weather this new storm.

*

Constable Lu didn't sleep at all on Saturday night, and precious little on Sunday. On Monday morning, he got up at first light and took the longest cold shower of his life. As he dressed, he checked his clothing – a recent article in *Socialist Youth* had said that this sort of thing could be caused by tight-fitting underpants. But they were as baggy as ever.

'Spiritual Pollution, that's what it is,' he muttered, and felt revolted at himself.

Yet as he took his bike out of the rack, he wished the old man from Flat 1406 as always up early doing his *taiji* a healthy 'Good morning!' And as he pedalled into town past the bright concrete towers of the Village built for last year's Asian Games and the ancient wooden gate of the Temple of the Earth, he found himself weaving in and out of the other riders as if he were winning a race. *Gold medal to China!* The sun was shining. The plane trees along the cycle lane were bursting into leaf – this thing called spring seemed to have more power than even ideology or love of country. As such, he knew he should be wary of it – but suddenly he couldn't bring himself to be so.

BE MORAL! a hoarding adjured him.

Yes, of course ... Those thoughts that had buzzed around his head all weekend were totally unworthy. He should be thoroughly ashamed of himself. Perhaps he should include a passage on the subject in his self-criticism. As he locked his bike into its rack, he hid his face from Mrs Li, the old lady who watched over the cycles during working hours. If she could read his mind, what would this fine veteran revolutionary say?

He found Bao already at work.

'Good morning, sir!'

The inspector looked up. His face looked worn as if he too had spent a weekend in turmoil.

'Found anything interesting, sir?'

'Not really. These other files just duplicate some of what Inspector Liu found out.'

'Oh ...' said Lu.

'Our operation was a success,' Bao went on. 'But we need another line of approach, too.'

Lu nodded his head, then an idea struck him. 'What about his daughter? Have you looked to see if there's anything on file about her? There might be some leads.'

'Hmm. Hadn't thought of that.'

'I could do some investigating if you like.'

'Yes, well, why not? I believe she sings under the stage name Jasmine. At the Qianlong Hotel, one of these big Western places. There'll be a file on the hotel; you could start there. And then ...' Bao's voice trailed away. 'She's an attractive young woman, isn't she?'

Lu blushed. 'Well, yes, sir.'

'Not the sort of girl you meet at pioneer camp.'

'No, sir. But I'm sure – with a bit of re-education …'

'Maybe she doesn't want re-education.'

'Not want?'

'Her father's probably a gangster. From what I can gather, a ruthless –'

'That's not her fault!' Lu exclaimed. 'If bourgeois influences persist in our society … '

'You stick to your work, Xiao Lu. Let the Party sort out the bourgeois influences.' Bao looked sternly at the young man, then felt guilty. It *was* a good idea, checking up on Ren Yujiao. He should have thought of it himself. 'OK. If you think it's worthwhile building up a dossier on Miss Ren, then go ahead. But be discreet. Discreet, understand, *ya*?'

'Yes, sir.'

Lu picked up a file and strode purposefully out of the office. Bao wondered if he was doing the right thing. But he was always complaining that too much initiative was stifled in the force. Give the lad a chance.

*

Bao spent the day at and around the People's Theatre, interviewing staff and vendors in the alley outside, showing them a photo of the murdered man and asking if they had seen him.

The woman selling tickets recognized the photo. She was sure he had only bought one ticket.

'Do you remember the mood he was in?' Bao asked her.

'Not really. There was quite a queue that night. I was busy.'

'But you remembered his face.'

'I've seen him here before. He's young. Most of the people who come here are old.'

Bao nodded. 'When he went these other times, was he always on his own?'

This, she didn't know.

A sweet-seller on the street outside recognized the photo, too. She had seen Xun talking to someone outside the building. Bao asked for a description of this person, but she said she didn't get a front view.

'Height?' Bao asked.

'Not sure.'

'Compared to Xun?'

'About the same.'

Bao nodded. One metre seventy-five. Tall for a woman or a southern male. Average for a Beijing man. 'Age?'

'I said, I only got a back view.'

'Clothes?'

'Jeans, grey *Zhongshan* jacket – and glasses. I noticed the hook round their ears. I don't know why, I just did.'

'I wish the rest of the public was that observant. Footwear?'

'I didn't see.'

'Male or female?'

'Male, probably. Short hair, anyway.'

'And the conversation. Was it friendly? Confrontational? Relaxed? Animated?'

'It looked... intense. I suppose that's why I noticed it. You pick up on things, don't you?'

'Some people do. "Intense" in what way? Friendly? Aggressive?'

'There was some kind of disagreement, as your young man was shaking his head violently at one point. But they kept talking. That's all I know. Sorry.'

'You've been very helpful. Anything else?'

'No.'

A photographer recognized Xun, too. He had posed for a portrait. With a woman.

'When?'

'About three months ago.'

'Can you describe her?'

'She seemed troubled. That's why I remember them. I usually get happy couples grinning at me. These were... different.'

'Physical characteristics?'

'Tall.'

'Tall? Attractive?' Bao added, suddenly making a link in his mind.

'No. Plain, actually. He was good looking – another reason why I remember them. Couples usually match.'

*

Constable Lu wheeled his bike up to the perimeter wall of the Qianlong Hotel and cast a quick glance over his shoulder. No one was looking. He hid the machine in a thorn bush and made his way on foot to the main gate.

'I can't do any harm,' he said to himself. A crow screeched; Lu's heart leapt, and he took some of those deep breaths Bao Zheng had taught him. Keep cool. This was going to be a combination of work and pleasure. Maybe he'd find some important clue – in a flight of fancy, he imagined himself sitting right behind Ren Hui and overhearing the guy say how he'd murdered this traitor at the opera. Would he arrest Ren there and then, or wait to tell the boss next day?

The pleasure element of the evening was obvious.

At the bottom of the hotel drive was a guard post. The occupant, whose job it was to keep Chinese out of this exclusive foreigners-only establishment, glared at the young man striding towards his window.

'What d'you want?'

'*Xing Zhen Ke*,' replied the young man, producing his identity card with a flourish.

'So?'

'Special mission,' said Lu.

'*Pei!* Bullshit!'

'I ... It's very ... Now, wait a minute –'

'Shall I phone your HQ to check?'

'No. I've said, it's a special mission.'

'What are you after? Export-only goods from the Friendship Store? Kick-back on the new pool contract? Or just a bit of bourgeois decadence up in the Starlight Suite?'

Lu was dumbstruck.

The gatekeeper began to laugh. 'Go on. If anyone asks, you climbed over the wall, OK?'

Lu grinned and walked off as fast as dignity would allow. The man returned to his magazine – *Shanghai Movie Pictorial* on the outside, a Hong Kong soft-porn mag on the inside – shaking his head and muttering about the age of policemen nowadays.

*

Jasmine Ren walked out on to the stage to the usual burst of applause. From the side of the stage, Eddie Zhang grinned up at her. The young floor manager's infatuation was as total and pathetic as ever. Who else was here? The spotlights didn't allow the singer to see too far into the audience, but Ken and Ray were both at their usual front tables. Alone with candles, ice buckets and champagne – French, of course, not the cheap, sweet Russian stuff the hotel palmed off on tour groups or local officials. She awarded both businessmen a smile before beginning her act.

'Welcome to the Starlight Suite,' she said in English then Japanese. 'I'm Jasmine, and I'm here to sing for you. Later on, it will be your turn to sing for me!' She turned and grinned at Ken, whose karaoke version of *My Way* never failed to reduce the band to laughter.

'I'd like to begin this evening with a song from America,' (time for Ray to get a special look).

More applause. The bass began playing a C, in a slow, heartbeat pulse. Drums joined in on kick-pedal and backbeat.

Jasmine felt a thrill run through her, the kind of thrill, she had decided, that only music could truly create. She was American now. She put her lips to the mike and let out a kind of moan that made even the barman stop and stare out at the stage.

After two sung verses, the guitar took a lead – another chance for her to scan the audience. Both Ken and Ray had expressed their admiration for her with compliments and presents. Both wanted to become her lover. Jasmine wasn't interested. She didn't have to take anything she didn't want. She knew how *baba* would feel, too. He hated her having any kind of boyfriend. But she went with a foreigner, he'd go crazy. *Baba* in his crazy mood was not something she liked to contemplate …

At the end of the number, the two businessmen tried to outdo each other in their applause. She thanked them with more flashing smiles. No harm in flirting, of course.

Outside, Lu walked up to the doorman and tried his ID again.

'There's no crime going on in there,' the doorman replied. 'Entry for non-residents is twenty-five yuan in Foreign Exchange Certificates.'

'Twenty-five!'

'Or ten dollars US.'

'Ten dollars! May I remind you that the People's Police have a right to –'

'This particular People's Policeman is trying to get into a very popular show without paying.'

'This is part of a criminal investigation.'

'D'you want a word with the manager?'

'No,' said Lu despondently. From behind the doors, *she* began to sing. The young man's insides seemed to tighten. The doorman noticed his expression and felt either pity or the opportunity for a special deal.

'Have you got *renminbi*?' he asked. People's Money, the money that ordinary citizens use.

Lu went through his wallet and held out the contents. The doorman counted dismissively through the grubby notes.

'Bring proper money next time. Welcome to Capitalism!'

That word was abhorrent to Lu. Capitalism meant selfishness, greed, disloyalty, immorality. But now it also meant hearing and seeing Jasmine. He slipped in through the door and joined his fellow-sinners.

*

The first set was over. Jasmine looked round at the audience again. She began to speak; Eddie Zhang tore himself away to put up the house lights.

'We'll be back again soon with some more music from around the world – this time, with your help.'

Ken grinned; he'd been practising. Jasmine lingered on stage to smile back at him. The lights went up. She lingered even longer. It wasn't just Ken and Ray staring up at her but the world. A big, rich world – men in thousand-dollar suits, women in dresses that cost years' wages for most Chinese. The one mainlander there – a young guy at the back, quite handsome, thoroughly embarrassed – stood out a mile for his feeble attempt to dress smartly.

There was something familiar about him.

'Come on, Jasmine. Off the stage,' the bandleader said. 'It's unprofessional.'

She obeyed, suddenly ill at ease. Where had she seen the young man before?

'Who cares?' she told herself as she retreated into her dressing room. 'He's just someone who's seen me around town, and who's found a back door into one of my shows.'

But she felt no better. The Starlight Suite was the one place where she was in charge. Who was this interloper? She would ask around.

Chapter Five

Constable Lu cycled home from the hotel in a troubled frame of mind. Ren Yujiao had looked him in the eye, he felt sure of that. But what had her reaction been?

Pleasure, at realizing that a proper Chinese citizen admired her work, not just a load of foreigners?

She hadn't looked that way. She'd looked... unhappy in some way.

Perhaps she'd read his feelings. Women were good at that, apparently. Maybe her natural modesty had been shocked by them.

No, her show wasn't exactly modest, but that was just a show ...

Or was it? Maybe she was truly immodest. So immodest that if they were alone together, she would –

'Watch where you're going!' shouted a fellow cyclist.

What worried Lu was the thought that she had been curious, and would want to find out more.

*

At work next morning, Lu felt this worry grow.

His duty that day was very dull. The boss wanted him to check more records – boring ones that revealed nothing. (The boss himself was working on that Triad file again. Lu bet that was a lot more interesting.)

All the more time for that worry to grow.

He had to find out more.

*

'Correct ritual is always followed.' Bao had underlined that sentence. Not assassination in an opera house. Yet the look on Ren Hui's face when he had mentioned Xun ...

He glanced up at the clock. Time to go home again. And to forget work for one evening. Forget, OK?

The inspector rode home through the diesel fumes and racket. Forget. He would cook a meal. He would do some *qigong* exercises. He would read. The new edition of *October*, the short story magazine, had just arrived. If the censors had got at it too much, he would go back to the classics. *Stories to Awaken the World. The Water Margin.* Or something more exotic, another one of those tales from that bizarre, far-off place called London, featuring the detection skills of *Fu Er Mo Si (Sherlock Holmes)*.

Bao's near neighbour Mrs Zeng was emptying a dustbin as he coasted into the compound of Tiantan Inner Eastern Building Twenty-six, the twelve-storey concrete block of flats where he lived. She smiled at him. 'Don't forget that dinner invitation.' The Zengs had been very kind since the business with Mei.

Bao pushed his bike into the rack and flicked its rear wheel lock shut. 'I won't. Work hours are so irregular at the moment. When this case is over …'

'You'll be on another one.'

Bao grinned. 'You're right. We'll fix a day. Next month. I won't be so busy then.'

He took the creaking lift up to the tenth floor, and made his way along the balcony past the strange assortment of objects that even Party members end up storing outside their doors due to lack of space. Flat 1008. Home.

By most people's standards, Bao Zheng's apartment was enormous. Four rooms, just for one man! A sitting room at least three metres square. A bedroom almost as large, its walls lined with books. A small kitchen and a stone-floored lavatory-cum-shower (hot water twice a day, morning *and* evening). Flat 1008 had, of course, once housed two people.

He sat down on the one easy chair and found himself staring at the photos on the heavy mahogany dresser. In one frame, three army sergeants shared a packet of *Double Nine* cigarettes and a joke, against the background of an out-of-focus Vietnamese jungle. Wan and Yi had both stopped bullets in the same action that Bao won his medal; Wan fatally, Yi to a long period in hospital, after which they had lost contact. Rumour had it that his former comrade had become moody, difficult and hard to employ. Next to it was a family group: Granny Peng, his father and mother, big brother Ming and little sister Chun, all dressed for 1 October celebrations in the late 1950s. Then a simple one of Bao in police uniform, his ex-wife Mei in a bright silvery dress from a Friendship Store.

Bao knew he should get rid of the last of these, but somehow the collection looked empty without it.

Mei had wanted more out of life than a man of Bao's background could offer. He had thought she would make him urban and sophisticated like her. She had... Well, Bao wasn't sure what she had seen in him. Whatever it was, it had proven an illusion.

Don't brood. Do something.

Bao enjoyed cooking as much as eating. He set the rice up to boil then prepared some pork, cutting the salty outer skin into cubes, searing them in oil and ginger then cooking them in rice wine, soy, salt and sugar. When these were nearly ready, he took off the rice, turned the power up to full and stir-fried some beans. A feast, all done on two rings of a burn-blackened mini-hob. He poured himself a glass of beer and ate slowly, savouring the tastes he had inveigled into the apparently simple ingredients. Delicious! A bowl of stock soup followed, then a mug of tea.

Work? Divorce? Forgotten!

To round things off, a little *qigong*. First, stillness. Concentrate on your own breath. In, out. Then begin to move. An extraordinary sense of deep calmness began to arise in him.

Bao had only had the phone fitted recently. Its bell made him jump. He grabbed the receiver.

'Who's that?'

Silence. Then a feeble, frightened voice. 'It's me, Lu.'

'Oh.' Bao composed himself. 'What's up?'

'I must talk to you.'

'OK. I'm listening.'

There was a sigh. 'Could we meet? I don't trust the phone. People might be listening.'

Bao gave a frown of puzzlement. 'Well, if it's that important...' He paused to remind himself of where Lu lived. 'Meet me at Zhengyang Gate in half an hour.'

He glanced at Mei again, and found himself feeling sorry for her, despite everything. Who would marry a policeman?

*

Bao stood by the southern gate to the old Imperial inner city. Soft music was playing from a nearby loudspeaker. The twittering of starlings in the gate's rafters competed with it. In front of him was Tiananmen Square, now largely dark and quiet. Dim ornamental lamps created isolated pools of half-light in its centre; around the edges, floodlights picked out the key points of the great buildings around it: the national emblem on the Great Hall of the People, the flag on the Bank of China, the portrait of Chairman Mao on Tiananmen itself, far away at the other end of the square. The grand boulevards that ran up and down the sides, that would have been thronged with traffic a couple of hours ago, were empty apart from a few bicycles and a colleague on a Japanese motorbike. A young couple walked past, hand in hand, a display of public affection that Bao still found puzzling. It seemed indecorous, somehow.

He lit a Panda and enjoyed the familiar, rich taste.

'Inspector Bao!'

Constable Lu came into view. The young man looked terrible.

'What's up?' Bao asked.

'I – I couldn't talk about it over the phone. Thanks for coming, sir –' Lu's voice died and his eyes fell to the ground.

'What on earth is it?'

'Well, sir, you know you told me to build up a dossier on Ren's daughter. Well, I was doing that, and ... She's disappeared.'

'Disappeared?'

'Last night I went to that hotel where she sings. To try and find out more about her.'

'I did say *discreet*, Xiao Lu. Did you find anything?'

'No, sir.'

'Did she notice you?'

'I'm ... not sure.'

'That means yes.'

Lu grimaced. 'This evening I went back there again – '

'You *what*?'

'I went back.'

Bao took a long drag on the Panda. To get angry would be to lose face. 'Why did you do that?' he asked calmly.

Lu looked at the ground and mumbled some answer about wanting to be sure whether she had noticed him or not.

'You're infatuated with her,' said Bao.

'What does that word mean?'

'You know bloody well what it means.'

'I suppose ...'

'Anyway, what happened this time?'

'Nothing. The performance had been cancelled. I asked why, and the doorman said Jasmine had reported sick.'

'People get sick. Even the young and irresistibly beautiful.'

Lu blushed. 'It – seems a coincidence.'

Bao sighed. He was always telling Lu not to believe in coincidence. 'This doorman. Did he know you were a policeman?'

'Yes, sir.'

'And who else did you play the "Let me in, I'm Public Security" stunt on?'

Lu stared at the ground again. 'The gatekeeper, sir.'

'Nobody else?'

'No.'

'That's something, I suppose.'

A truck backfired on Qianmen West Street, sending the starlings whirling into the night sky. Bao battled with his emotions. 'You were a fool to go there in the first place,' he said finally, 'and a complete fool to go back. But you have been brave to come and tell me now. Well done for that. The operation might have been compromised. We must act fast.'

*

When Bao knocked on Meng Lipiao's door and no one answered, he told Lu to kick it down. The constable leant back and brought his boot down just behind the lock. The door splintered and yawned open. The two officers burst into a dingy bedsit. Bao's heart sank as he contemplated the clothes on the floor and the disarrayed bed.

'Too late!' Bao felt the anger at his young colleague rising again – but with it a callous professional pleasure. This surely showed they were on the right track.

A head peeped up from behind the bed.

'Oh. It's you,' it said.

'Yes. Why didn't you answer when we knocked?'

'I was busy,' said Meng. He stood up, draping a sheet around his naked body. 'You've damaged my door.'

'We'll send a man to repair it. If we'd have been the *Yi Guan Dao*, it would be more than your door that got broken.'

That look of instant terror again. 'They've found out what I told you?'

'No. But there's been, well, a hitch in our surveillance operation. I'm not taking any risks. So get dressed and packed.'

'Where are you taking me?'

'Somewhere where you'll be safe.'

'Jail? Just because you dogs can't keep a secret?'

'Because I keep my word. It's no problem for the *Xing Zhen Ke* if you get sliced up and dumped in the Tonghui River by Ren Hui and his friends. But I've got a conscience.'

Meng looked at Bao suspiciously. He distrusted all policemen, especially when they started talking about conscience. But he feared the *Yi Guan Dao*.

*

Giddy from the lift, the inspector stepped out on to the twentieth floor of the Qianlong Hotel. He padded across the thick crimson carpet to the doors of the Starlight Suite and went in. There was a bar by the door, tables and chairs in the middle, and a stage at the far end, crammed with the impedimenta of Western 'music': drums, electric keyboards, amplifiers and microphone stands. A middle-aged woman was polishing the bar-rail. She glanced up at the new arrival, scowled and got back to work.

Bao made his way to the stage and hopped up on to it. Lu said he had been standing in the far left-hand corner. About where the cleaner was now. Ren Yujiao could have recognized him easily.

Backstage was a tatty dressing room, along whose near wall were coat racks with sequinned costumes on rusty wire hangers, and mirrors with light sockets above them, mostly empty. A door led into a smaller room that was carpeted, well-lit and sweet-smelling. Two bouquets of flowers sat in vases. Bao bent down and read the labels, one in Western writing, the other in Japanese.

He felt a tingle at the back of his neck. Policeman's instinct: he was being watched. He turned to find a burly man with a scar on his chin standing in the outer doorway.

'Can I help?' said the man aggressively.

Bao smiled back. 'I don't know. Are you part of the band?'

'No.'

'Ah. I hear they put on a good show.'

'They do. Very good. What's it to you?'

'I was wondering … I've always wanted to hear Western music. Is there any way you could get me a ticket?'

The man sneered. 'You'd better speak to Mr Zhang.'

'And his office is … ?'

'Down the corridor, third right.'

'Thanks,' said Bao. He took one more look round the room, just to show the big man that he would leave in his own time, then left.

*

The young man with fish-bowl glasses grinned nervously as 'Inspector Gao' introduced himself.

'I'm Eddie,' he said in reply, pointing at a plastic badge on his lapel with English writing on it.

'And your Chinese name?'

'Kangmei. Zhang Kangmei.'

Bao smiled. He didn't usually approve of people taking Western names, but this seemed a reasonable exception. Kangmei – Resist America! – had been fashionable in the late 1960s, when this young man would have been born. But it wasn't ideal for someone showing the Qianlong's guests to their 400-dollar-a-night suites.

'How can I help you, inspector?'

'I've heard good things about the show here.'

Eddie grinned nervously. 'Yes. Jasmine is the most talented singer we've had in this place. Ever!'

'I'd like to come and see her.'

'Ah. That might be … She's taking a short break at the moment.'

'Any reason why?'

'No, just … ' The young man paused. 'Actually, seeing as you're a policeman. I was wondering … ' He stared down at the desk. 'I know it sounds silly, but, well, she didn't turn up for work last night. She's never done that before. She's a real professional. I've seen her knocked out with 'flu, and still go up on stage and give a wonderful performance. Wonderful. And when she went through all this business with that boyfriend … But last night it was a simple call. "I can't make it this evening. Sorry." That was all she said. That's not like her, officer. Not at all.'

'People sometimes act out of character.'

'I rang this morning, too, but got no answer. I don't know what's happening.'

'May I have the number, please?'

The young man frowned, but did as asked.

Bao noted it down. 'Has she been acting strangely recently?'

'No. If anything, she's been extra cheerful.'

'Do you know why?'

'Not really. Women have moods, don't they?'

'Do you think she got a better offer from another venue?'

'She was doing so well here!'

'Maybe an offer from abroad. So much popular entertainment seems dominated by foreign influences, nowadays.'

'Jasmine was a good patriot. She had no wish to go abroad.'

'Did she have admirers?'

Eddie blushed. 'She was a very attractive woman, so, yes. There was a Japanese and an American. But I don't … Do you think she has run off with one of them? I don't see that, officer, I really don't.'

'You could check if they are still resident here,' Bao suggested.

'Good idea! I'll do that straight away!'

Bao smiled. If only every police interview went this well!

'She never did anything, you know, immoral with them,' Eddie went on, as he dialled reception. 'She wasn't that type.'

'Are you sure?'

'Well, I – yes. I am sure. I got to know her well. She confided in me.' Eddie beamed with pride. 'She needed someone strong in her life. Strong spiritually, not the crass kind of men that tried to pursue her.'

He then broke off to ask about the two guests, both of whom turned out still to be in residence.

'Who else was significant in Ren Yujiao's life?' Bao asked once the call was done. 'Anyone: Chinese, Western.'

'Well, there was me.'

'Of course.'

Eddie fell silent. 'And, well – there was the boyfriend. That didn't last, of course. He wasn't good enough for her. A low type of person, by all accounts.'

'What was his name?'

'I don't know. She never said. She said it had to be kept a secret.'

'Did you ever see him?'

'No.'

'And he never came to the show?'

'Not to my knowledge.'

'That's a little odd. Perhaps he didn't like Western music. D'you know when they first met?'

'No. They were already together when we took Jasmine on, and that was three months ago.'

'And when did they split up?'

'26 February. I'll never forget it. She was in tears; she said she wanted to die; she had a kind of fainting fit five minutes before curtain-up. Then the show began, and she went on and gave a marvellous performance, even by her standards. Inspector Gao, you should have been there!'

Bao bit back a comment about the shows being for foreigners only. 'Tell me about any other people in Jasmine's life. Any female friends?'

'I never met any. I think she preferred male company. Women can be very envious.'

'And the band?'

'Friends – but no more. They all, er, desired her, of course. I'm afraid musicians have very low minds.'

Western ones did, thought Bao. 'Tell me about Jasmine's family. Her father for example.'

Eddie glanced away and said nothing.

'This discussion is in confidence,' Bao went on.

The bespectacled eyes found his again. They were afraid.

'If you want me to help, you must give me as much information as you can.'

Eddie nodded. 'I never met him. I know he had a lot of power over her. And he had a reputation as a violent man. I did once declare my, er, admiration for Jasmine. Next day, a great lout came round with a message from him, that he would kill me if I so much as touched her. I tried to explain that real love needn't involve all that physical stuff, and that my feelings were of a spiritual nature. The fellow just snarled at me and repeated his threat.'

'But you never met this man? He never came to see her show, or to talk to any of your colleagues?'

'Not to my knowledge.'

Bao picked up a pencil and began whirling it round in his fingers.

'How did Jasmine first get hired here?' he asked, after a long silence.

'Mr Li appointed her.'

'Who's Mr Li?'

'Our Brand Profile Manager.'

'What does that mean?'

'He runs all the entertainment, decides on the decor of new rooms, what sort of items we sell in the hotel shop, that kind of thing.'

'Ah. He doesn't have a scar on his chin, does he?'

'Oh, no,' Eddie replied. 'That'll be Chao.'

'Ah. Who's Chao?'

'I don't really know. He's a maintenance worker or something. He hangs around the suite a lot – I'd love to get rid of him. I want the Starlight Suite to be a place of magical beauty. People like him lower the tone.' He sighed. 'We need Jasmine back here. Officer, I'm so grateful for your time. I really am worried.'

'I can see,' said Bao. 'I am grateful for your assistance. If you have any further information … '

He took out a card and wrote his false name and real number on it.

Chapter Six

When Eddie Zheng rang next morning, Lu took the call.

'Inspector Gao? I think you've got the wrong – Oh, that Inspector Gao. You must be Eddie.' He wasn't supposed to say that, either. Never mind: the guy was jabbering into the phone and probably hadn't even noticed the slips.

'So let me get this clear … ' Lu said, once a break came. 'Your boss has said that you have to find a permanent replacement for her.'

'That's right.'

'He must be crazy. She's … I've heard that she's very good.'

*

'It could be coincidence,' said Bao. 'But I know what you're going to say, and you'd be right. We'd better go and pay Mr Ren a visit.'

'Right!' said Lu.

'Or … maybe someone else should.'

*

Eddie Zheng stood in the street, staring at the door. Her door.

When someone answered, he was to say that he was from the Qianlong and to ask if he could speak to Jasmine. The aim was to find out why she had left, 'so they would know not to make the same mistake again'. That was the line.

He'd been reluctant to do this at first. What would Mr Li say?

But the inspector had been insistent. This was the best way he could help Jasmine. And it might even have the effect of persuading her to return. If Eddie could just get across how eager her fans were …

Now, here, outside the door, he felt the fear coming back. He thought of the thug who had threatened to kill him.

'It's my responsibility to get her back on that stage,' he told himself. 'My stage. As soon as possible.'

He walked up to the door and gave it good, hard knock.

No reply.

He knocked again.

'Anyone there?'

And again.

'This is important.'

Still no reply.

Eddie was suddenly unsure what to do. Wait a little longer? He did so, feeling ever more embarrassed.

'I'll come back in half an hour,' he told himself.

*

'We've had a barrel microphone on the place for 24 hours,' Bao told his boss next day. 'It's empty. We need to search it from top to bottom,' said Bao.

'You'll still need permission,' Chen replied down the crackly line from Huashan. 'Apparently Mr Ren ... has connections.'

'How long will that take?'

'I don't know.' Chen paused. 'Can you go in more ... undercover?'

'I thought you didn't approve of such activity.'

I think that ... in such exceptional circumstances ... '

*

Nobody looked twice at the two men in baggy Mao suits and scuffed trainers entering the dingy *hutongs* of Chongwen. The taller, younger man was pushing a cart – he was obviously some kind of vendor – and the other had a canvas bag slung over his shoulder.

'This is the place, said the older of the men, who was Bao Zheng.

The other, Constable Lu, parked the cart and they went and stood under a wall. When nobody was about, he made a cup with his hands. Bao placed his foot in it and heaved himself up.

'*Tamade!* Glass.' He pulled off his cord-lined jacket and laid it across the jagged pieces of old bottle set into the top of the wall. On a signal, Lu pushed extra hard. In a moment Bao was over the obstacle and had dropped down into the corridor below.

'Now that's good for a 40-year-old!' he muttered to himself, and made his way into the courtyard proper. The black outline of Ren Hui's house stood out against the pink glow of the city sky. Bao let his eyes accustom themselves a little more to the darkness.

He tiptoed across the yard to the annex window, took out a can of sweet-smelling gum, smeared it over the windowpane and pressed a folded jute cloth on to it. After a minute to let the gum harden, he took a cutter out of the bag and began working round the window frame. The little motor sounded like a chainsaw to him, though he knew it was inaudible more than ten paces away. When the job was done, Bao pulled gently at the cloth-fold and the pane slumped into his hands. He shone his torch through the hole.

He took three deep breaths and checked his watch. Still forty-five minutes till the area's lights came back.

Inside the house, he padded into the hall – the bolts on the front door, Bao remembered, had been fastened from the inside – then into the room where Ren had received them. He ran his torch round the walls.

Everything had gone.

Carpets, jade, tapestries: anything that he had noted as being of worth. Even that horrible, butchered drinks cabinet. Bao gazed around in astonishment, then set to work on the few remaining items of furniture. A filing drawer rolled open; it was empty. A drab, modern desk had been searched but left full of bills, correspondence and cuttings about Jasmine's musical career – Bao bundled them into his bag, though he doubted they'd be of much use.

A utility room contained various electrical goods and a shelf full of drink. Beyond it was a small, simply furnished music room. Another quick search: nothing of interest.

A board creaked as he made his way upstairs. Bao berated himself for treading too heavily. 'I'm still good at this stuff,' he told himself, thinking of how easily he'd got over that wall, and how skilfully he'd taken the glass out of that window.

He worked through the rooms thoroughly. Ren Hui's bedroom was sparse. Had a painting been taken down from the wall? His wardrobe was half full: the best outfits had been taken. The bathroom yielded nothing of interest.

This door had to be to Jasmine's room.

A tiny part of Bao felt a slight unease at prying into a young woman's world like this. The rest of him was a policeman doing his job. He pushed the door open.

A Western pop group of indeterminate gender posed above her desk; European and African models in huge hats and minute skirts grinned and pouted round the walls. Jackie Chan stood guard at the door.

Jackie hadn't done a very good job. This place had been ransacked. Papers lay everywhere, drawers hung open. A clasp file marked 'personal' lay pathetically open. Bao sat down on the bed and began to read through it. Poetry in English, possibly words to songs; some work, signed as her own, in Chinese.

The cranes are calling in the mountains,
The wind answers through the pine trees,
The deer runs free in the forest.
In the city, young men and women are fasting for freedom.'
It was dated 27 May 1989.

Three symbols of longevity, then youngsters risking their lives. Nice. Ren Yujiao might be the daughter of a Triad Enforcer, but underneath she was clearly a person of sensitivity and intelligence. He wondered how deeply she had been involved in the events of that turbulent month. Had the mess in this room been caused by the *Ke Ge Bo*? If so, he should back off, now.

He had a job to do. Bao turned his attention to the singer's desk. It was unlocked. Inside were a clutter of cassette tapes, more poetry, letters and photographs. He gathered these up and put them in the bag.

An inner drawer was half-open. Bao pulled at it, and it wouldn't budge. His curiosity aroused, he tugged harder and harder, until it finally popped out. A sheet of cardboard that had been wedged down one side flopped into view. On it was a montage, of a photograph and a newspaper cutting, the latter dated 4 January.

Sparkling Performance at People's Theatre

From time to time, even the most respected pieces of repertoire need a fresh approach. Last Thursday, the troupe Shengli from Tianjin gave a dazzling new interpretation of Lady Zhaojun ...

'Aha!' said Bao. The photograph showed Jasmine and a man holding hands. They were standing in Dazhalan Alley, about a hundred yards from the theatre, and the man was Xun Yaochang.

Bao put the card in his bag, then shook his head and transferred it to his jacket pocket, next to his notebook. He did the same with the poem. Then he sat down on the bed and thought.

Plain, that photographer had said ...

He returned his attention to the file and ran through the poetry till he found a more recent verse.

Bright lights sink into the bitter sea;
The bird of love flaps its wounded wings
How much strength has it left?

28 February, this year.

'Our charmer joins the Triad. Seduces the daughter of one of its top men. *Baba* finds out and is not impressed. Then what? Does he send a hitman to get him out of the way? Possibly. But why at the opera?

Did *she* kill him? That would make more sense of the location, which was the oddest aspect of this case. He is told to ditch her and does so. She misinterprets this and, a spoilt child, gets revenge. Bao shook his head. Would her dad have taught her such precise execution skills? Maybe she'd learned them anyway. Maybe the opera location made some kind of perfect revenge for her? Deranged people could do that sort of thing.

No, too far-fetched.

So why there?

Bao looked down at his watch. These operations should be carried out as quickly as possible.

Going downstairs, that board creaked again.

'OK, I'm a little out of practice.'

It was an easy climb out of the window. He put the glass back, though wondered if the owner would ever return. The Triad would not like the fact that personal feelings had imposed on business. He began to walk across the quad.

Running feet. Several sets. For a moment he couldn't work out where they were coming from. Then he could – but it was too late. He felt a punch in his ribs and arms grabbing at him.

'Police!' he called out – but he was wrestled to the ground and kicked.

'Gimme that bag,' said a voice. (Local accent, male. Middle-aged?)

'This is state evidence…' Bao began, but another kick sent pain searing through his body. He grabbed the bag extra tightly – but a third kick made him let go. The evidence was gone.

'Fucking dogs,' said one of his attackers. Bao tried to grab hold of the speaker's leg, but he suddenly found all movement excruciatingly painful. The man aimed a kick at him.

'Don't move!' called out a voice. 'Police!'

A gunshot rang out. The men ran.

Chapter Seven

Bao watched as a nurse in a round, white cap hurried past, her heels clicking on the stone floor. Down the far end of Ward Five, International Peace Hospital, a young lieutenant who had had his leg blown off in a training exercise was having another of his fits.

The occupant of the bed next to Bao's, a colonel in Political Education here for a gall bladder operation, tutted. 'Noisy bastard,' muttered the old man, then went back to his comic book.

'You have a visitor.' The voice belonged to Miss Lin, the Ward Sister.

'Oh. Zhao! Good to see you.'

'You are looking rough,' said the new arrival.

'I'm feeling much better!' Bao replied, aware that Miss Lin was still watching them: she was a great believer in 'the power of a positive attitude'.

Miss Lin seemed to realize she was intruding and walked off.

'I've brought you a present,' Zhao added, once the Sister had gone. He handed Bao a small bottle of Yantai brandy.

'My favourite!' Bao took a sip. 'This is a marvellous present.' Another sip. 'Quite marvellous!' Then he heard footsteps, and slipped the bottle under his pillow. 'What news from work?'

'Everyone's been saying what a great job you've done. It's the talk of the department.'

Bao looked puzzled.

'She's confessed to the murder. Didn't you know that?'

Bao sat up with a jolt, gave a cry of pain and sank back on to his pillows.

'The photo you found clinched it. Secretary Wei put out a warrant for her arrest, but she walked into a station in Dongcheng yesterday and handed herself over.'

Bao pulled out the bottle and took a swig. 'Handed herself in?'

'You know how much more lenient courts are with people who admit their own guilt. Even in murder cases.'

Bao sank back on to his pillows. 'It doesn't feel right. Too far-fetched.'

'Sometimes our "feel" is wrong, Zheng.'

'But the MO. It was so professional.'

'She was a gangster's daughter.'

'Nobody saw a glamorous young female at the theatre.'

Zhao shook his head. 'I don't know the details. Criminals can be good at disguising themselves.'

'Even her long hair? The one witness said the killer had short hair.'

'You can hide anything if you want to badly enough.'

'I guess so.' Bao sighed. 'It still makes no sense. And how did those bastards know I was in Ren's house?'

Zhao gave a shrug. 'Maybe they also had mikes on the place. I'm sure you were as quiet as you could be, but … '

'But what?'

'Covert work like that is a young man's job, Lao Bao.'

Old Bao. The inspector shook his head, then sighed. 'They broke two of my ribs, you know,' he said, keen to change the subject.

'Bastards.'

'How's Lu?'

'Back on duty. Upset. Secretary Wei gave him a dressing down for "bourgeois sentimentalism".'

'He did a good job rescuing me. Wei ought to find someone his own size to pick on. Any hope of catching those fuckers?'

Zhao grinned. 'There's no evidence. Clever of you to get Lu to bring a gun – though they won't like it on Zhengyi Lu.'

'They can go to hell.' Bao hated the fact that the headquarters of the Internal Security Bureau, the *Ke Ge Bo,* were in Justice Road.

Zhao smiled. 'I'd have done exactly the same on a mission like that, too. So would any working policeman. Chen needs you back on the Huashan case. He'll get a memorandum from the ISB; he'll make a little speech then forget all about it.' Bao's colleague shook his head. 'You're lucky. You're in favour at the moment. I got a roasting for my self-criticism.'

'Your … ? Oh, that.'

'They let me rejoin in the end, of course.'

Bao had forgotten about 'Strengthen the Party'. He told himself again that it would all be OK, then began searching for a new topic. Then Miss Lin appeared, smiled at Zhao and pointed to the ward clock.

'I'm sorry. We have to be strict with visiting hours. Come a bit earlier next time.'

'I shall,' Zhao replied with a smile. He turned to Bao and winked. 'D'you think they'd let me in here for a few days?'

Miss Lin laughed. 'You have to do something brave and patriotic first.'

The colonel grunted and turned over another page of his comic book.

*

Next day, it was Lu's turn. The young man handed over a box of dried plums in liquorice and one of those trashy novels about Martial Arts masters.

'I didn't see anybody,' he said. 'Not a soul.'

'I'm sure. There must have been another way in. We just didn't spot it. You did well. Those thugs wanted to give me a good kicking.'

Lu's instructions had been to keep watch over the place, to apprehend anyone trying to enter, and to move in if he heard any suspicious noises by putting the cart against the wall and climbing over. Bao had also told him to bring a gun, but to only use it in extreme necessity. Firing it pretty much at random hadn't been what his superior had had in mind, but it had at least scared the attackers away. Apprehending them would have been better, but maybe Lu had been right …

'Thank you, sir.'

Silence fell.

'So you're getting better?' said Lu.

'Slowly. Ribs take time to mend. And there's bruising. No serious internal damage, fortunately.'

'Very fortunate, sir. An old person like yourself … Not that you're that old, of course,' Lu added hastily.

'Thank you, Xiao Lu.' Bao paused. 'I have to ask you – did you tell anyone about this mission?'

'No, sir. Of course not!' Lu's look of horror at the very thought was obviously real.

'Just asking.'

'Why would I do that?'

'You wouldn't, but – I needed to hear that from you.'

Silence fell. 'You know she's confessed, don't you?' said Lu.

'Yes. Don't let it upset you.'

'I'm not upset. She was a bad element.'

'I thought you were going to re-educate her.'

Lu blushed. 'That's a job for the state, isn't it?'

'The bird flaps its wings and is gone.'

'Sorry?'

'It's a poem.'

'Ah. I don't really read poetry. It's not very manly, is it? D'you think I should?

'Only if you like it.'

*

Next day, Team-leader Chen came to visit, without a present. 'Well done!' he said in a loud voice. 'Our team is the talk of the department. Secretary Wei made a personal visit to the office the other day to offer his congratulations.'

'That was nice of him.'

'We can't wait to have you with us again,' Chen went on. 'Your skills will be in particular demand.'

'I'll be back at work as soon as I can.'

'Good. It's urgent.'

'It will take some time, though.'

'Of course. But there is a lot of work to be done.' Chen lowered his voice (the colonel in the next bed leant over to listen and nearly fell onto the floor). 'You shouldn't have let Lu take a firearm on the mission. Given the circumstances, I shall overlook the matter. But rules are rules. When can you start?' he continued in his loud, official voice again. 'Next week?'

'They say a rib takes six weeks to heal.'

Chen looked horrified. 'There have been two more thefts,' he said out loud, then returned to his whisper. 'Things are getting serious. We need all the manpower we can get!'

'Haven't the constables been doing the filing properly?'

'I'd, er, like you to come and join the team at Huashan. On-site investigation.'

Bao's expression lightened. At least some good had come out of the Xun affair. He wondered how far he could push his new-found favour. 'I want to do some investigating of my own.'

'Policing's a team business. What had you in mind?'

'To take a little time to look around the site. To talk to the people who work there.'

'Everybody's been interviewed. Several times.'

'I know. I've read the transcripts. But this would help me settle in. That way, I'll be able to get back to work quicker.'

Chen looked at him suspiciously. Then sighed. 'What sort of time did you have in mind? Next week?'

'I'll do my best, comrade Team-leader.'

'Thank you, Xiao Bao.'

Chen had to head off for an important Party meeting. Bao watched him go. No, surely, Chen couldn't have told the Triad about the raid. Unless, of course, those men weren't from the Triad in the first place …

*

'No visitors today?' said Miss Lin.

'No.'

'Haven't you got a family?'

'Not here. I'm from Shandong.'

He scanned the Sister's face for disapproval – many Beijingers look down on *xiang ba lao* country people. He saw none.

'I was married, but I'm not any longer,' Bao went on. 'My ex-wife lives in Shanghai.'

The ward sister nodded thoughtfully. 'Oh, well, we'll look after you here.'

When she moved on to the next bed, Bao allowed himself a longer look at her. She really was a most attractive woman.

He enjoyed the thought – he'd cut such stuff out of his mind since the spilt with Mei, and it was pleasant to be aware of desire, or at least admiration, again. Not that he had any hopes of taking that any further, of course. Back in Shandong, a woman of Miss Lin's beauty would have married ages ago. Here in the city, she no doubt had a 'boyfriend' or enjoyed the attentions of a string of admirers. Still, it was nice to feel the pleasure again.

*

Bao reported for duty at HQ a week later. He sat on his familiar chair, staring round at his office. The maps, the cabinets, the striplight, now emitting a low persistent buzz. And, of course, his calligraphy scroll. *Zheng Yi*, justice. He thought of the Xun case.

It's solved, he told himself. I've done well.

He shook his head.

When Chen appeared from a sub-committee meeting, Bao told him that he wanted to see Ren Yujiao again. Chen's usual post-Party-business grin collapsed at once.

'You can't be serious. Why?'

'There are one or two details that I have to clear up. It's important.'

'So is our work at Huashan. Anyway, this isn't a Public Security case any longer. It's all in the hands of the People's Prosecutor.'

That evening, Bao put a call through to the People's Prosecutor.

*

Ren Yujiao sat huddled in a corner of the cell, on a hard wooden seat next to a half-eaten bowl of rice. Gone was the *qipao* and Western make-up of 'Jasmine'.

'I'd watch out, sir,' said the warder, closing the grille. 'She's a wild one.'

'Thank you,' Bao replied coolly. 'I know how to look after myself.'

The door swung open and he walked in. His nose wrinkled at the smell of sweat and damp.

The prisoner barely glanced at him. 'What d'you want?' she mumbled.

'Just to ask a few questions … My name is Bao. Bao Zheng.'

'I've said everything, haven't I?'

'Have you? Everything?'

'Everything.'

Bao paused. 'So you really killed Xun Yaochang?'

'Of course I fucking did. It was what he deserved. Cheating little shit … ' She looked up for the first time in the interview – Mei's eyes – and her expression changed at once. 'I've seen you before, haven't I? Where was it? Oh, yes. You came to do business with my father just before all this happened.'

Next moment the rice bowl was hurtling past Bao's ear, and Jasmine was on her feet screaming at him.

'You made all this happen! You pig! You monster!'

Bao would normally have tried to calm her down, but he was not in a fit state to take physical action – a last resort, of course, but a necessary back-up. He began to back off. Then the door then flew open and two warders rushed in.

'If you come here again, I'll kill you,' shouted Jasmine. 'I've killed once. I'll do it again.'

'I did warn you, sir,' said the taller of the warders as they locked the door behind them.

'Yes, you did.' Bao shook his head sadly. 'I guess I'd better leave her to you.'

*

When he got up to his office, he began clearing his desk of all the documents relating to the Xun Yaochang murder. Once they were in a neat pile, he took them over to the waste paper bin. Then he put them down on the floor and cleared some space on a shelf for them.

He still felt connected to the case. Maybe it was the physical pain it had caused – and was still causing, though he was getting better every day.

Maybe it was also a rather literary kind of sadness. Xun and Jasmine had both been better than the crummy environments in which they had found themselves. Her tainted, ultimately crushing privilege. His simple poverty and foolish ambition. Classic tales of doomed love came to his mind. The 'Butterfly Lovers', Liang and Zhu.

'There's more to the story,' he told himself.

Then he reminded himself how often cases ended like this: the basics clear enough but loose ends flapping in the wind. His collection of black notebooks (one for each case) contained many of these.

And there was work to be done.

Chapter Eight

The Volkswagen Santana Shanghai came bumping out of the spruce trees, crunched along the dirt road of the upper valley and stopped outside the barbed wire enclosure. Sergeant Fang, at the wheel, tooted the horn. The noise echoed along the massive rock faces all round them. Nobody appeared.

'Hoot again,' Chen said from the back.

The sergeant did so. More echoes. Then a gatekeeper ambled into view with a mug of tea in his hand. Chen wound down the window and shouted at him to hurry up. The man mumbled something uncomplimentary under his breath.

'They should pay us more respect,' said the team-leader.

Bao Zheng, who was sitting in the front next to the driver, stared up at the landscape ahead of him. A huge grey granite triangle jutted up out of the head of the valley, with a diagonal slash of sandstone across its face that made it look as if it had been in a fight with a knife-wielding giant. Huashan, Flower Mountain – such a pretty name for such a stark place. The slash, of course, was what made Huashan special: it was the site of the caves. Eleven hundred years ago, towards the end of the Tang Dynasty, a group of monks had fled here to escape the persecution of the Emperor Wu Zong. Bao tried to imagine their feelings, to enter this valley, see the red scar and know it would be pitted with natural sheltering places.

The Shanghai bumped down the rutted passage between the compound's neat rows of tin-roofed huts, pulling up outside one with a sign on the door: THE PEOPLE'S POLICE SERVE THE PEOPLE!

'Ten minutes to relax, then we prepare ourselves for another round of interviews,' said Chen, stepping stiffly out of the car on to the hot, rocky earth.

'Waste of time, those interviews,' muttered the fourth member of the team, Inspector Zhao, once Chen was gone. Bao was inclined to agree, but fortunately that wasn't his problem, for the moment, anyway. He got out, stretched and took in a deep breath.

'Cigarette?' said Zhao.

Bao told himself this was his chance to give up. Remember that recent directive? In these surroundings, he could fill his body and his spirit with fresh, clean mountain air.

'Yes, please,' he said.

The two policemen lit up and stood looking round the walls of the valley.

'It's a beautiful place,' said Bao.

'I guess so. You stop noticing after a while.' Zhao, one of the few members of the team who did not need to wear glasses, rubbed his eyes.

'What's the view like from up there?' Bao asked.

Zhao shrugged. 'Hills, valleys, mountains. There's usually a haze.'

'Classic Chinese landscape!'

'Well, there aren't any willow trees or Daoist monks moping about, but I guess in a way you're right.' Zhao shook his head. 'Give me a nice modern scene any time. Motor cars, decent houses, electricity.'

The two men took some more puffs.

'So you really have no leads at all?' said Bao.

'Not a thing. We've got filing cabinets full of work rotas, inventories, timesheets, roll-calls, day-books, night-books… Nothing seems to add up. We've had the phones here tapped.

We've followed site-workers on leave. We do spot checks of people and vehicles in the vicinity.'

'And none of the missing items has ever been seen again?'

'No. Well, except for that Buddha that went on sale in New York. What was the asking price? Twenty thousand US dollars? Thirty?' Zhao shook his head. 'That's hundreds of thousands of yuan, for a bit of stone.'

Bao nodded. 'And there are no suspects?'

'Nobody and everybody. Chen, of course, says this person is a Party member so can't be guilty; that person once made a joke about the Four Modernizations so is a prime suspect. Any serious investigator who looks at the facts remains baffled.' Zhao took a final drag on his Panda then threw the stub onto the earth. 'Welcome to the insoluble mystery called Huashan.'

*

The path up to the caves made no concession to comfort. It was sometimes a steep slope, sometimes rough steps, and never free of rubble despite the efforts of two soldiers whose job it was to keep it clear and safe. Bao's ribs began to ache about a third of the way up. He pushed on for another third, then sat down for a rest. The view was already spectacular. The compound below had become a toy, and peaks were beginning to emerge over the valley walls. In the distance, pine trees marked the narrow mouth of the valley, through which the dirt-track was the only exit to the outside world. No wonder this place had guarded its secret so well for so long.

'ID?' said a guard when Bao reached the top of the path.

The inspector fumbled in his pocket and produced it.

'That's fine, sir. Carry on.'

The first of the caves had been of no archaeological interest, so had been commandeered by Security. It now had bunk beds, a short wave radio, a gas stove, and a supply of water in a plastic barrel. A calendar featuring Shanghai movie starlets added a touch of homeliness. Underneath it, a shaven-headed teenage recruit sat filling in a notebook in slow, carefully formed characters.

'That's the day-log you're doing, is it?' Bao said to him. 'Mind if I have a look?'

'We're not supposed to show them to anyone, sir.'

'Not even police investigators?'

'I just do what I'm told, sir.'

'Give it to me. That's an order.'

Each watch kept logs, which were collected and compared at regular intervals. Bao had read dozens back in Beijing, but this was the first he'd seen on site. It was no different to the others. A mystery noise on the upper path, which had turned out to be a rockfall. A porter on the path attacked by an angry eagle. A sensor in Cave Fifty-four triggered off by bats ...

He leafed back to the beginning and began reading.

An entry in red. Theft, reported 09.35 hours. Site, Cave Sixty-seven. Object, stoneware figure of the goddess Guanyin, height 212 mm.

Bao shook his head. He'd seen pictures of this piece, one of the finest finds on the site.

'You search everyone coming off the mountain, don't you?'

'Oh, yes, sir.'

'What's the exact procedure?' Bao asked, more out of habit than in hope of any great revelation: the searches wouldn't need to be very thorough to reveal items as large as the missing Guanyin. He let the young man demonstrate, then thanked him, went back out onto the narrow walkway that led along the fault-line and connected the caves.

PAY ATTENTION TO SAFETY! said a sign. It wasn't really necessary. Bao had nothing to his left but a drop into the valley of over a hundred metres. He smiled; he had no fear of heights as long as his feet were on solid ground, and few things were as solid as Huashan.

Cave Five was the site of some wall carvings, one of which had been carefully removed by Professor Qiao and her team, then stolen. Cave Twenty-two was famous for its frescoes, still, fortunately in place. Bao would go and look at them another day when he had more time. In a gesture worthy of Chairman Mao, the cave next to it had been turned into a latrine.

Cave Forty-four was the largest, but the monks hadn't used it. Possibly they'd counted the caves, too; the words for *four* and *death* are so similar. Professor Qiao's modern, superstition-defying team had made it their headquarters. The site hoist operated from outside it. Inside Cave Forty-four all finds – ones that hadn't been stolen, anyway – were carefully wrapped and prepared for their journey to the valley floor. Right now, there was nobody about except for a small, round man in a sunhat, busy polishing the already spotless housing of the hoist motor. This individual needed no prompting to talk.

'Everything important comes up or goes down here. Food, water, tools, empties, artefacts …' The man gave the housing a fatherly tap. 'Sit down. Another half hour or so, and you'll see it work.'

Bao offered the man a Panda, lit one himself, and dug in for a long monologue. He wasn't sure that watching a hoist pull a box up on to a mountainside would tell him much, but at this point in an investigation it was wise to gather as much information as possible. Seemingly irrelevant things could later turn into leads.

*

'This reminds me of a job I did on a site in Beijing,' the hoist engineer was saying. 'There were considerable technical problems, all of which I managed to overcome, of course … '

Bao's mind was already elsewhere. What other means of transportation were available to the robbers? Some hidden route through the caves? Hardly likely. The path? It ran on up the fault-line, right to the mountain's south-west ridge, apparently. Did it continue round the other side? Supposing –

A buzzer was sounding.

'That means ready!' said the operator. 'Watch this!' He pressed a button on the motor, and the two hawsers that had been curving gently down into the abyss began to straighten.

'What kind of weight will this be?' Bao asked.

'Average is two hundred kilogrammes. More sometimes. You'll be amazed how much stuff has to come up.'

'And go down?'

'Of course.'

The box left the ground. If the payload was as great as the operator said, the additional weight of a small statue would not be noticed.

The box remained tiny for most of its journey, then was suddenly life-size and a metre or so away. Two students came out and grabbed it. Bao followed them into the cave and watched it being unloaded. Nothing of interest emerged, just drinking water, bottles of chemical for the latrines and diesel for the site generator. Even so, the whole process was carefully overseen by two security men. Once the job was complete, Bao spoke to them.

'You always watch the unloading this carefully?'

'Oh, yes.'

'And the loading?'

'Well, of course.'

'How much d'you know about Tang Dynasty Buddhist art?'

The men grinned; they'd probably been asked this question before. 'If there's anything old, one of the experts does the inventory.'

'Any expert in particular?'

'Not really. Dr Jian is up here most often, so it's usually him.'

'Ah ...' Dr Jian was the second most senior academic on the site. Team-leader Chen regarded him as a major suspect. Jian had been heard criticizing the Party several times, often broke regulations, had missed a police interview because he was 'busy' elsewhere, and generally showed signs of bourgeois individualism.

Bao ran slowly through the system of record-taking with the guard. Loads were listed in triplicate; a copy was kept here, two sent down with the box. Down there, they'd be double-checked; later they'd all be married up and compared. The system appeared foolproof.

'Can you recall a time when the loading wasn't observed?' he asked. 'A time when someone senior told you to get out?'

'No, sir.'

'You're sure?'

'Oh, yes.'

Bao walked over to the hoist box and checked it for a false bottom or sides. 'How many of these boxes are there?'

'Don't know. Only one, I think.'

He watched as an archaeologist began refilling the box with shards of pottery, describing each one in detail before wrapping it up in a page from *Enlightenment Daily*. When the box was full, the senior man summoned the students to carry it out. The hoist motor began running again and the valuable cargo sank from view.

Some other items, it seemed, had not been so fortunate.

*

About half way along the sandstone fault was a small outcrop of rock. The caves beyond this were too small to be of archaeological interest, and the site's chief security officer, a man named Wu, had declared this upper section of the path out of bounds. A clutch of red characters daubed on the rock like a political slogan reminded people of the fact. There was nobody guarding the outcrop, however, and no physical barrier. Bao walked straight by on to the forbidden upper section.

The path grew even narrower almost at once. The inspector glanced down at the valley floor. Wu had been quite right to prevent people from coming up here. Nobody would survive that drop. He pressed on, and the path soon widened out again.

There were still caves to his right. All too small for the monks to have lived in, but still big enough for someone to crawl into and hide things. A brief examination of one of them showed a tinder-dry interior – no wonder objects lasted so well up here – and fissures of rock heading off in all directions. The thought of a secret passageway down off the mountain came back to him, though exploration revealed that this cave would not be the start of one.

Back in daylight, he dusted down his uniform and carried on up the path. He finally reached the top of the fault, where the sandstone intersected the mountain's south-west ridge. The path came to a sudden end, in another sheer drop. Bao paused. The only way on was up the ridge, to the summit. It didn't look too hard or long a climb – though the price of a mistake would be high.

Bao had the skills, but was he fit enough? He sat down, and gazed at the sawtooth mountains that now rose up all around him like a frozen sea. To the north, he could see the Great Wall switchbacking its way along the horizon. Bao told himself that in such a magnificent setting, the superior man can only excel himself.

It took him less than ten minutes. The ridge forked and levelled off to form a long flat gully between two spines of rock a few metres high, like the crown of a molar tooth. He was at the summit of Huashan. The inspector lit a Panda and enjoyed his achievement to the full.

'*On mountainous ground I position myself on the sunlit heights and lie in wait for the enemy.*' The quote from Sun Zi came to him in an instant. The summit was a perfect fortress, walled and with only one access route.

It was also invisible from both the lower caves and the camp, which gave Bao a feeling of relief. Sometimes you needed space and silence to think properly.

'Hey!' Two men were on the upper path. One had field glasses trained on him, the other was shouting.

'What's the matter?' Bao called back.

'You're not supposed to be up there!'

'Oh.'

'Come down!'

The inspector thought of arguing back, but there suddenly seemed little point. He made his way slowly down the ridge to where the men were waiting.

'You need permission to go beyond that outcrop,' said the one with the field glasses, pointing back down the path.

'Who from?'

'CSO Wu or one of the team-leaders. Didn't you see the notice?'

'I've got a job to do,' Bao snapped, then reflected that he needed all the friends he could get in this investigation. 'I'll get clearance next time,' he added.

The guard looked mollified. 'This path gets very narrow in places.'

'I've noticed.' They began to walk back down. 'So – how often do you patrol up here?' Bao asked.

'Quite frequently.'

'Because people quite frequently come up on to this section without permission?'

'Yes. Especially the archaeologists. You can't tell those fuckers anything.'

'Any archaeologist in particular?'

'Jian. He's forever digging around in the caves up here. It would suit us all fine if he fell off – but it's our job to stop that happening.'

'So you stop and reprimand him?'

'Of course. A few days later he's back here again. I'm afraid he has contacts in high places.'

'Does Dr Jian come up here alone?'

'Sometimes. Other times he brings a couple of the students with him.'

'But you've never, well, caught him with anything illegal?'

'Illegal?'

'A missing artefact, anything like that?'

'No. It would be great if we did.'

They walked past a cave, and Bao peered into it. You could hide hundreds of things in there.

Chapter Nine

Dinner at site HQ was supposed to be a communal affair. In practice, eaters sat in groups: police, site security, archaeologists, porters, maintenance workers. Bao collected his bowl of noodles, cabbage and bean-curd, a purple preserved egg and a steamed bun. He found a table where he could sit alone and watch people.

The fortyish male, surrounded by a gaggle of students, had to be Dr Jian. His audience listened intently as he spoke – Bao couldn't follow the monologue exactly, but it was something about a conference in Europe.

The old lady sitting alone, immersed in a book propped up against a water-jug, had to be Jian's superior, Professor Qiao. Her face was lined – she was in her sixties, now – but her expression was one of contentment. It was an expression Bao had seen before on the faces of people who had undergone great suffering at an earlier time in their lives, of the kind that either broke people or made them. He knew her story. At the height of the Cultural Revolution, a gang of Red Guards had smashed their way into the professor's home and pushed her husband off their fourth-floor balcony. Qiao had been marched through the streets in a dunce's cap, locked in solitary confinement for a year, then set to clean lavatories in the institute where she had been a senior lecturer. She had always been a loyal Party member; her husband's crime had been to have criticized Chairman Mao ten years earlier, during the brief liberalization of the 'Hundred Flowers' campaign.

The power of the past, Bao thought. Ironic, in this place dedicated to discovering and treasuring the past.

Among a table full of security men, Bao recognized from a photograph their chief officer. Wu was ten years younger than Qiao and had done a number of relatively easy security jobs before this one. Bao was shocked by how old this man looked. The CSO could hardly hold his chopsticks. It was bad enough investigating these mysterious crimes, he thought. How would it feel to be responsible for preventing them in the first place, and failing so miserably?

Or, of course, what would be even more stressful still would be committing the crimes and having perpetually to cover up.

A man in a beautifully-tailored Mao suit, also eating alone, had to be the Party man here, Team-leader Hei Shou. Hei was nominally in charge of every aspect of the operation, but Bao sensed he had little control over anything official. He looked as distant as the professor, but lost in his own thoughts rather than a book. He didn't seem the type to go scrambling up mountains, but was in the perfect position to monitor and protect others doing that job.

There were, of course, fifty other people in this room, slurping the unappetising canteen food. Any one of them could be responsible – even one of Bao's own colleagues (though the thefts had started before they had been called in, so that was unlikely). However, he had a feeling that someone senior had to be involved. Someone who could pull rank in a difficult situation.

But he could be wrong. There were tables full of fit young men and women, who probably wanted more out of life than an academic's or a soldier's pay could provide.

Bao turned his attention to his food. It was getting cold. As it probably would have been revolting anyway, did that matter? He tore a piece off his bun. Proper *mantou* bread should be sticky, but this was as dry as the summit of Huashan.

He reminded himself that he had asked to be transferred here, and began to eat.

*

'Busy day's work tomorrow,' said Team-leader Chen.

Bao nodded. The two men were walking in silence back to the police accommodation hut – a silence that was neither companionable nor strained, just silence. When they reached it, Bao stayed outside to smoke a cigarette, then went to find his quarters, a cubicle with thin plywood walls. It was enough; it gave him sufficient privacy for him to sit on his hard bed, gather his thoughts and then take out his notebook.

First, a page for each suspect (everyone was suspect). Then apply 'the method'.

Everything relevant.

What is known and what is presumed.

The 'pressure points' and what action should be applied there.

There seemed to be no answer to the last question. He sat, pencil whirring through his fingers, pondering what might be.

'Somewhere a crack will emerge,' he said finally.

*

Bao found Dr Jian next morning cataloguing pieces of broken pottery in the long main workroom. The young academic scowled when asked if he 'would like to answer a few questions' and said that he did not want to do so in front of his subordinates. It was demeaning.

He and Bao went for a brief walk to the perimeter fence. Despite the early hour, it was already warm: when summer came, this would be a harsh place to live and work.

Bao tried to introduce a note of informality into the conversation. 'I often find it easier to talk in the open air, anyway,' he said.

'If that means our conversation will be shorter, that suits me,' was Jian's reply.

Bao ignored the comment. 'I understand you sometimes venture beyond the official limits of the dig.'

'Is that what you've dragged me out here to talk about? Regulations? I get enough of that from the chief security officer. I expected something a little more stimulating from Beijing *Xing Zhen Ke.*'

Bao smiled. 'I'm interested why you make these expeditions.'

'I'd have thought the reason was obvious.'

'Tell me, anyway.'

'I'm an archaeologist. My business is looking for artefacts.'

'But the monks never lived up there.'

'They were fleeing persecution. It's very possible that they hid things there. Special, sacred things. If you knew anything about history – '

'Have you found any artefacts there, Dr Jian?'

'You know I haven't. But that doesn't mean there aren't any. There are a lot of caves on the upper section.'

'It must be very time-consuming to search them all. Have you discussed this extra activity with your superior?'

'Professor Qiao and I have a good working relationship. She trusts me enough to let me follow my intuition.'

'And your team-leader?'

' "Comrade" Hei Shou? He knows nothing about archaeology. What's the point in talking with him?'

'How about your students?'

'I talk to them a great deal. That is my job, or part of it, anyway. Look, I don't understand where all this is leading.'

'I'm just trying to get facts sorted out. I also happen to find the subject of your work interesting.'

Jian turned to his questioner. 'Interesting?'

'I read one of your papers. "Is the political and moral decline of the late Tang Dynasty reflected in the period's art?" I didn't understand some of the technical terms, and I don't have the knowledge to engage with the arguments. But I appreciated the piece, and it has added to my appreciation of the era's culture.'

'An intellectual … ' muttered Jian.

'My father was a peasant, but had a respect for learning. I believe your own background is not dissimilar.'

Jian nodded.

'My business here is to stop the thefts,' Bao continued. 'I would like your help in that.'

They walked on in silence for few minutes, then Jian began to talk. He said how he was busy in the main caves most of the time, but occasionally went past the outcrop on to the upper pathway. He was working his way slowly up towards the summit. So far he had searched the eight lowest out-of-bounds cave systems. He had in fact found a few scraps of pottery, but had not announced the fact as they were of no value.

'I sometimes wonder if the security personnel here want us to succeed,' he went on. 'They seem to have found a perfect way of combining minimum effectiveness with maximum interference. *Don't go here! Don't do that!*'

'They have responsibilities.'

'They enjoy interfering. They even spy on us. I know Wu watches through a telescope. The phone is tapped. And only the other day, I was working late on a report and there was a noise at the window – I turned round and someone was running off.'

'The guards patrol the compound all night, don't they? It was probably just one of them, bored and a little curious.'

Jian shivered, as if even the memory of the incident scared him. 'Maybe. But I wish they'd catch this thief, not go round frightening people.' The young academic glanced down at his watch. 'Look, Inspector Bao – I'm sorry if I was rude earlier.

You've probably seen how things are here. Everybody suspecting everybody else. It gets to you. From time to time, your team-leader sits me down in his hut and virtually accuses me of the crime.'

'He's only doing his job. But I accept the apology.'

'Good.' Jian looked at his watch again. 'Can I go?'

'Yes.'

Jian turned away, then back again. 'I've say this to your team-leader every time, but he doesn't understand. You might. The objects being stolen – some of them are national treasures. That statue of Guanyin, for example. It's China's. Our heritage, our soul. No Chinese archaeologist could steal it and sell it to the highest foreign bidder. If you knew the history of the subject in this country – the damage inflicted by White Russians and Americans at Dunhuang, the destruction we brought upon ourselves during the Cultural Revolution – you would know that. Such a thing is unthinkable.'

The young man turned and walked off, leaving Bao to ponder if he should recommend him for this year's Golden Rooster awards, best actor category, or if he had been sincere.

*

Chief Security Officer Wu's office was in a hut in a far corner of the camp, from which he had the best view of the mountain. Bao knocked on the door. A voice told him to come in; when he did so, he found the CSO peering through a telescope at the mountain-face. Wu turned towards his visitor.

'How can I help you?' Wu said, with such coldness that Bao was taken aback.

'I, er, just want a few words. About the section of the pathway above that outcrop – the section you put out of bounds.'

'What about it?'

'I gather people still go up there.'

'I can't stop them. I'd have to have men on guard there the whole time to do that. I don't have the resources. That's not my fault.'

'No ...' Bao let his eyes rove round the hut – simple unadorned walls, the telescope, a sniper rifle in one corner. 'I also want to talk about the thief.'

Wu's eyes widened. 'You know who it is? Congratulations. It's taken you people long enough.'

'I'm afraid not. But I was wondering if *you* had formed some view as to his, or her, identity.'

'I might have done.'

'Care to share your thoughts with me?'

'Not really.'

'I gather my team-leader, Chen Runfa, hasn't made himself popular by his interrogation methods. Forthright, I believe he is –'

'Accusatory.'

'But you must see that everybody has to be under suspicion. You're a security man; you must understand that.'

'There's suspicion and suspicion. Chen interviews people as if it was 1972. *You are guilty! Disprove it!*'

Bao nodded. 'You're talking to me now, not him.'

'So? You're all the same, you Beijing big shots.'

Bao, who knew the CSO was a countryman, said, 'I'm from Shandong, actually.'

'You've lost your accent.'

'Not totally,' Bao said defensively.

Silence fell. Bao let it.

'You asked for my opinion, so I'll give it to you,' Wu said suddenly, 'It's one of those archaeologists. It either has to be one of them or one of my men, and I trust my people. We have security clearance, too; they don't.'

'There are others on the site with minimal vetting, Bao put in. 'What about the porters? Or the man who operates the hoist?'

Wu shook his head. 'I also think our thief is clever. An intellectual. What did the late Chairman call them? "The stinking lowest rank of humanity." Your team-leader should spend less time harassing honest members of the working class and more time investigating those chicken-fuckers. That's my view.'

Bao nodded. Wu had given the problem thought after all; he wasn't as stupid as he tried to make out, even if he did seem to equate intellectualism with homosexuality. 'And how do you think the thief gets the stolen goods off the mountain?' he asked.

'Smuggles them, I guess. My men don't always get to search the top people as rigorously as they should. Party members can cause trouble for an ordinary soldier trying to do his job.'

'But quite large items have disappeared.'

'Maybe those go at night. If I had enough men, I could mount a proper twenty-four-hour guard.'

'Nobody would walk that path without lighting at night, surely.'

Wu shrugged. 'Someone's getting the stuff off the mountain.'

Bao nodded. Only one piece had appeared in the international art market. Maybe the rest was still up on the mountain somewhere. 'Who determines the size of your guard?' he asked.

'I do. Within my budget. That's the problem. How can you protect a site like this with such little money?'

'And who determines the budget?'

'Hei Shou, the big Party man.'

Bao nodded. Maybe there was a larger context for all this. Did someone right at the top want the project to fail? Or was someone up there ultimately profiting from the thefts? Silence fell again, which Bao used to look around Wu's office.

'Mind if I have a look through your telescope?' he asked.

Wu didn't seem keen on the idea, but said: 'OK.' The security man got up and began fiddling with the eyepiece. 'It's a good scope,' he said finally. 'Look, there's Engineer Wang polishing his bloody hoist motor again. You can even see the smug look on his face.'

Bao put his eye to the mechanism. He ran the telescope along up the path, past the rock outcrop to the upper section, past those small caves, one of which he had crawled into, until the curve of the mountain's face took the fault out of view and there was nothing but sky.

As a boy, he'd been fascinated by the stars that shone clear and bright over Shandong Province. He'd told himself one day he'd get a telescope and explore them. Then other stuff had come along in his life.

'D'you have a radio link up to there, too?'

'Yes, but it's not reliable. I've complained about it enough times, but nothing gets done. Hei Shou again. I wonder what he does in that hut of his all day.'

'Have you ever spotted anything odd through this telescope?'

'Yes. Archaeologists, wandering up on to the most dangerous part of the pathway. No protection, no precautions. That bugger Jian's the worst.'

Bao waited for Wu to say more, but he didn't.

'But you never see people loitering suspiciously around the theft-sites?' Bao said, after a pause.

'Sometimes. I send a man to check. It's always turned out to be harmless.' Wu cleared his throat and spat into a bowl on his desk. 'The thief is clever. Bloody clever. An intellectual, you see. He has to be. But he'll make a slip one day. Intellectuals always do.'

*

Bao knew a little about Team-leader Hei Shou. Before being given the job of archaeologists' team-leader, Hei had been in charge of a factory. Quite a famous one: Shenchun Number Three Machine-Tool Factory had been one of the first enterprises in the People's Republic to be declared bankrupt after such things were allowed at the end of the previous decade.

He had been exonerated from any blame. His predecessor had run Number Three on 'outdated' lines. Bao could imagine what that meant: big character posters exhorting workers to produce more; piles of unwanted machinery rusting in a yard outside. He wondered why Hei's factory had been at the top of the list for closure. Had he been particularly inept or just unlucky? Or had there been criminal activity there? By the boss?

'Come in,' said the team-leader when Bao knocked at his office door. Bao did so. Hei's desk was piled with papers. 'Sit down. How can I help?'

'I want to talk about money.'

Hei looked surprised. 'Money?'

'What sort of budget does this operation have?' Bao asked. 'And is it keeping to it?'

The team-leader sat up and straightened the line of pens in his top pocket. 'The People's Government attaches the highest importance to archaeological research, as part of the development of Socialist Spiritual Culture. However, in the current economic situation, financial controls must be exercised in all areas of activity –'

'It's in trouble, then,' Bao interrupted.

Hei's face twitched and a look of exhaustion filled it. 'It's these robberies. Everything's behind schedule. Beijing wants to close the whole operation down. We will seal up all the caves and smash the path up the eastern flank. Maybe in twenty years, there'll be the resources to begin again.'

'Who knows about this?'

'Me. Professor Qiao, who approves, as she thinks the job isn't being done properly any longer. And now you.'

'Nobody else?'

Hei shook his head. 'I wouldn't tell any other academics. It doesn't concern Wu and his men. And none of your colleagues has asked.' He paused. 'The thefts have meant more expenditure on security. Savings have to be made elsewhere. Work has had to slow down. And everybody blames me.'

'More expenditure on security?'

'Yes. I'll show you the figures if you like. Judging from your surprise, you have been talking to CSO Wu, who says we don't spend enough. But we have a budget to keep to.'

Bao nodded sympathetically. 'How much does it cost to run this operation?'

'Around fifty thousand yuan a week. It's not sustainable.'

Bao shook his head. 'Tell me about Dr Jian,' he said after a pause. 'Nobody seems to like him much.'

'His colleagues do. He's an up-and-coming star. Very bright and all that. But he hates the likes of you and me. I guess it's all to do with – well, you know, all that business on Tiananmen Square. He reckons anyone who's in the Party is directly responsible.'

'He seems to be able to get away with making trouble.'

'He's got contacts in high places. People who admire his work. Apparently, he's a Marxist, and there aren't many of those left in academia. I thought we were all supposed to be Marxists – but what the hell do I know about universities?'

Bao nodded again. 'How did you get this job, then?'

Hei grinned. 'I don't really know. I was seconded from the Finance ministry. I had a nice job back in Beijing…'

'Your family are there?'

'Yes. Well, my son is in America, studying. Economics,' he added. 'Not ancient pots and wall paintings.'

Expensive, Bao thought. But Hei didn't have the look of a man concealing anything.

He reminded himself that looks can be deceptive.

*

'Time to stop,' said Inspector Zhao as he packed away for the evening.

'I'll be along shortly,' Bao replied, looking up from the pile of files he had spent the last two hours working through.

'What are you checking?' asked Zhao.

'The phone monitoring.'

'What about it?'

'Who knows which phones are bugged and which ones aren't?'

'In theory just us, Hei Shou and CSO Wu. But you know how it is – you can tell, if you're alert.'

'The thief would be alert.'

'Ah – so you *do* have a theory.' Zhao peered over his shoulder at the files. 'Dr Jian? Have you got something on him? That would be a perfect solution. Arrogant little shit.'

Bao snapped the file shut. 'My investigations are at a very early stage.'

'Lucky you. Mine have been going on for months and got nowhere.'

Bao grimaced. He knew how fortunate he was, being able to follow his own leads and intuitions, not tied down by Chen's obsession with routine. Reading those reports, he found himself wondering if the team-leader wanted the thief caught at all.

'Let me buy you a beer in the canteen,' he told his colleague. 'Just give me another ten minutes.'

Zhao's expression lightened at once. 'Deal!' he said, and left.

The office door shut. Bao read on a little – some female students had complained that someone had been snooping on them. One reckoned it was a pervert.

Bao shook his head and glanced up at the clock. He tidied his desk and put the files back in the green steel cabinet. The key turned easily in the lock. Who else, he wondered, had keys apart from himself, Chen and Zhao?

Questions, questions; he had had enough for one day.

*

Music came floating out of the mess room, another of those sentimental Taiwanese ballads about lost adolescent love. Bao really didn't like this stuff. Another sign of age? But he headed on towards the lights of the building anyway.

The drunkard staggering round the corner nearly bowled him over.

'Watch where you're going!'

The man glanced at Bao, then turned tail and ran. On impulse, Bao gave chase. The man dodged and dived, then fell. Bao stood over him.

'Get up!' he ordered sternly. Then, when he saw who it was: 'Are you all right?'

Chief Security Officer Wu got unsteadily to his feet. 'You won't report me, will you? Not a fellow countryman. City folk don't know how to drink! Please.'

'You can rely on me,' Bao replied. The chief smiled, shook him overzealously by the hand, then stumbled off into the darkness.

Chapter Ten

Usually, after he had drunk a bit, Bao had the same dream, of running from a phalanx of armed soldiers but getting no further away from them. Last night, he and Zhao had put away several Tsingtaos and a tumbler of Maotai spirit, but Bao was dreaming of food. A bowl of decently-cooked rice, sea-cucumber stuffed with minced pork and ginger, deep-fried Yellow River carp in black rice-vinegar sauce. Then a siren started up, barging its way into his feast like an uninvited guest. It wouldn't stop; the meal was a memory; he sat up and rubbed his eyes.

Outside, figures were running. Bao threw on his uniform and staggered out into the early morning air.

'What's up?'

'Accident,' said someone.

A crowd had gathered by the gate. He went over to join them.

'One of your people,' said another spectator. 'Fell off the mountain.'

Bao, instantly cured of last night's excess, ran back to the investigation office. It was locked. His imagination raced. It wouldn't be Chen; the team-leader rarely left his office. If anyone went up the mountain, it was usually Zhao or Fang.

Zhao appeared. 'What's it all about?'

'Don't know. Someone's fallen off the cliff.'

Zhao raised his eyebrows. 'Had to happen, didn't it? Those stupid bloody archaeologists!'

'It's one of ours, apparently.'

'What? Who?'

A party of men could be seen approaching the camp. The two policemen walked down to the gate, arriving at about the same time as the stretcher-bearers. The body was covered with a sheet.

'Where are you taking him?' asked Bao.

'Don't know, sir,' one of the men replied. He looked pale and his breath smelt of vomit.

'Use the main workroom,' said Zhao. 'They'll have to stop fiddling with bits of pottery for the day.'

A man ran ahead to warn Professor Qiao. Bao walked alongside the body.

'Who was it?' he asked the stretcher-bearers.

'We're not quite sure.'

They cleared a space in the workroom and put the body down. Bao pulled back the cover. Dr Jian, who had been watching with interest suddenly ran out of the room. Bao grimaced, thinking he recognized the victim. He went through the pockets. He'd been correct. It was Chief Security Officer Wu.

The man who had found the body was a Private Han. When Bao suggested he show him the place where he'd made the discovery, the lad looked less than enthusiastic.

'You'll have to get used to the sight of death if you're going to be a soldier,' Bao said as they walked across the dry upper valley.

'Yes, sir,' Han replied. He was lanky and delicate featured, not really the fighting type. Bao seemed to recall that Han came from a good family. They had probably pressurized him into joining up.

Bao took him through his story again. 'You'd gone for a walk, and heard a scream. You looked up, and saw Wu falling. Correct?'

Han nodded.

'Did you look up to check where he'd fallen from and if there was any activity up there?'

'No, sir.'

Bao hoped the lad wouldn't try and transfer from the Army to the police.

They reached the scree at the foot of the mountain. Han pointed to a small, jutting rock caked with blood, now dried black.

'It was here, sir.'

'Yes.' Bao glanced up at the mountain. 'Is this where he actually hit the ground? A falling body can bounce or roll quite a long way.'

'Don't know, sir. I didn't see him land.'

The inspector began to clamber around the scree slope. He soon found a bloodstained dent in the pebbles. He thought of the body again.

'Thank you, Private Han. You can go. I'm sorry to bring you back here so soon.'

The young man scurried off. Bao worked his way methodically around the area, but found nothing. Then he turned and walked back to his hut through the gathering heat.

*

The plastic barricade tape flapped noisily in the wind. Bao stood with a two-man patrol, peering over the edge of the precipice from the point where, it was assumed, Wu had fallen. A long way.

'No one's tidied up here, then?' he asked the patrol's leader, a sergeant.

'No, sir. Mr Fen gave strict orders to leave everything untouched.' Fen, Wu's deputy, had stepped smartly into his boss's shoes.

'Good. And the orders have been followed?'

'As far as I know, sir.'

'Excellent.'

The path had its usual thin cover of dust and pebbles. No signs of a struggle. At the edge, a short section of newly exposed rock appeared to tell what had happened. Wu had been standing too close to the edge, on an overhanging lip that had given way.

Why stand there? The path was over a metre wide at this point.

Maybe he had still been suffering the after-effects of last night's drinking. But why come all the way up here in that state?

'Who else was on the mountain early this morning?'

'Just us and the boys down in Cave One.'

'You're sure?'

'As sure as I can be. I didn't see anyone else. Zhang didn't, either.'

The junior man confirmed his superior's comment with a nod.

'But you saw the chief?' said Bao.

'Yes,' the sergeant replied. 'He just walked by.'

'Did he look agitated?'

'No more than usual. He was always jumpy. These thefts got to him. I guess he felt they were his fault. And he had a chip on his shoulder about cities. He was *xiang ba lao*, a real shit-shoveller. He was determined to show us city folk he was better than us.'

An image sprang into Bao's mind, of the hardworking people among whom he had grown up. He suddenly wanted to get a shovelful of shit and empty it over this bloody townee. 'So Wu put in a lot of extra hours, patrolling the upper section of the caves on his own?'

'That's right, sir.'

'And that is what he was doing when he fell?'

'I guess so.' The sergeant shrugged. 'Who knows what he was up to? Shit-shovellers are all crazy, if you ask me.'

An eagle flapped past. It was a welcome diversion. The junior soldier seemed fascinated by it. 'I've got this theory,' he said suddenly.

The sergeant glared at him.

'What is it?' Bao asked, as much to annoy the sergeant as out of genuine curiosity.

'I think he was attacked by an eagle, sir.'

'Zhang ... ' the sergeant warned.

'No,' said Bao. 'Let him speak. What makes you think that, Young Zhang?'

'Well, Comrade Inspector, they get vicious if you go near them. Especially this time of year, when the chicks are in the nest. I've often thought, if one of them attacked you, and you were on that path, you could easily lose your balance and fall.'

The sergeant kept glaring.

'Interesting,' Bao said.

'Eagles are intelligent birds, Comrade Inspector,' the young man went on. 'I read this piece in the *People's Daily* last year. Party cadres in mountainous Shuangfen County had trained eagles to deliver handwritten messages from village to village, thus saving valuable resources of fuel.'

'Couldn't they use telephones?' said the sergeant.

'Don't know. Perhaps there weren't any. It didn't say in the article.'

'They were probably too stupid to operate them.' The sergeant launched into an impromptu comic turn, of a man with a thick rural accent trying to figure out a telephone and failing.

'You have an intelligent young man here,' Bao told him at the end, pointing to the sergeant's subordinate. 'You should listen to what he has to say.'

*

On his way back, Bao met his colleague, Inspector Zhao, heading the other way.

'Anything worth seeing up there?' Zhao asked.

'Not really. I really think he just fell off. He liked to drink.'

'Poor sod. Anyway, I've been told to come and find you. We have a lead.'

'Really?'

'They've found another of the stolen pieces.'

Bao gasped. 'Where?'

'In Guangzhou.'

'Guangzhou?'

'A tourist was trying to smuggle it over the border to Hong Kong.'

'Hong Kong?'

'Chen's delighted. He wants us all to move down there. All the top people, anyway.'

'That seems a bit of an overreaction.'

'Seek truth from facts,' said Zhao. 'At last, we actually have one.'

'Guangzhou...' Bao muttered. 'Such a long way away. They need a network to get it there...'

Was this the 'pressure point' the investigation needed?

*

Chen was on the phone when Bao entered the office. The team-leader gestured to him to sit down, then resumed his conversation.

'No, I don't think that would be a good use of public funds. Simple accommodation will do us fine. A barracks? Perfect. An officer in the People's Police doesn't require luxury.'

'Zhao's told me the news,' said Bao, when the call was over.

'Good, isn't it?' said Chen enthusiastically.

Bao nodded. 'I'm just finalizing arrangements. Zhao is the only linguist among us,' Chen went on, a slight sneer in his voice at the word *linguist*, as it implied taint from foreign influence. 'He'll be going to Hong Kong. Bao, you and I will base ourselves in Guangzhou. Sergeant Fang, Constables Lu, Tang and Han will remain at their current posts. We leave here at 05.30 hours tomorrow morning. Estimated time of arrival at Qianmen East is 08.00.' Chen grinned. 'I knew this would happen. Wait long enough, and criminals always make a mistake.'

*

The alarm, hidden under Bao's pillow, went off at half-past one. He lay in silence for several minutes, listening for signs that it had woken anyone but him. Chen's snores from behind one partition gave a clear message; Zhao, on the other side, was a heavy sleeper anyway.

He got up and dressed: a tracksuit, trainers, gloves.

The night was muggy, warm and still. He trod carefully: sound carried here.

Chief Security Officer Wu's office was a long way from their quarters, right out by the perimeter fence, but Bao passed nobody on his way there. When he arrived, he sat on the step and listened. The silence of Huashan valley was as absolute as it must have been eleven and a half centuries ago.

The new security officer, Fen, had had a thick steel padlock fitted to the door. Bao didn't recognize the type, but he had plenty of time. He took a wire from his pocket and set to work. The moon went behind a cloud. Bao glanced up. Still no one about. Back to the lock. Two more clicks and it sprung open. Bao grinned with pride at his handiwork. Could anyone else on the site have done that?

Apart from a chair that had moved and a stronger smell of alcohol, Wu's office was as Bao had remembered. He walked to the telescope and peered through it, but it was pointed at an empty piece of sky. He sat at Wu's desk and began working through its contents.

'This will all be tidied up by the time we get back from the South,' he said to himself. 'I either get to see it now, or not at all.'

The papers on the top seemed undisturbed. Bao put them in a lozenge-shaped pool of moonlight on the hut floor and began to read.

Memorandum, to Deputy SO Fen, re rockfall, Section Fifty-eight.

Report from Patrol Three, re failure of routine test of bleepers.

Security clearance for maintenance engineer to check hoist motor.

Sickness and overtime sheets for week ending Sunday 19 May.

Bao worked through the pile, then glanced at his watch. Half-past two. The perimeter guards usually set off about now. He slid the papers out of view and waited.

Two thirty-five.

Two-forty. Come on, boys ... Then he heard the sound of boots. Someone cleared his throat and spat. A shadow fell across the window. For a moment, the inspector felt a strange, unwarranted tingle of fear, then the shadow was gone, and the footsteps receded.

Next, the desk drawers. They opened easily. The first contained inventories of finds, cave by cave – useful for the thief, but exactly what a security officer would need, too. The next contained rough paper and a notebook in which duty rosters had been worked out. Wu had divided his men into three categories: circle, square and triangle. Circles and triangles usually worked one of each in a team. One good man and one poor one? Good information for a thief, but good security practice too. Read on.

Chen Runfa, Team-leader. A triangle.

Bao Zheng, Inspector (Second Class). A circle. And yesterday's date.

Bao began looking for patterns. Any correlations with dates and times of thefts? No, of course not. But why should there be? A theft could go several days without being detected.

Still, it was worth noting any obvious patterns.

When he had finished copying the significant combinations from Wu's notebook, he cleared out the drawer: just a few scraps with characters jotted on. Take *Corp. Hu off nights. Double guard, Cave Fifty-three.* One piece of paper had figures on, 6321275. A phone number, Bao guessed. He took the paper and stuffed it into his pocket.

The last drawer was empty.

Five to four. Chen and Zhao would be stirring soon. He put everything back as he had found it, took one last glance around, then tiptoed across to the door and left. The lock clicking shut sounded uncomfortably loud, but the noise was swallowed up by the silence.

The moon hung low over the mountains as he made his way back to his own quarters. The tin roofs of the huts glowed in its light, and there was a faint smell of resin from their unpainted wooden sides. The cry of an eagle echoed across the stillness. This could be such a beautiful place, he thought. Man makes it ugly, with his greed and suspicion, and now with death.

Chapter Eleven

The airliner gave a lurch. A grinding noise filled the cabin. Combat Hero Bao Zheng closed his eyes and said a prayer to the ancient God of War.

There were more bumps, more metallic groans, a sudden deceleration, a revving of engines. The hero's last thoughts were of that ward sister in the hospital. Then the plane's canned *erhu* music went dead. So the end would come in silence …

'A most enjoyable flight,' said Team-leader Chen. 'Most relaxing. Our national airline does a splendid job.'

Bao opened his eyes. The plane was taxiing across the tarmac. 'So do our national railways,' he muttered.

The aircraft came to a halt and a ladder was wheeled up to the side. The passengers began to disembark, each one recoiling as they stepped out into the heat. By the time Bao reached the tarmac, he could feel his body tickling with sweat. And they still had to walk to the terminal! Then the outline of a car appeared in the haze. It acquired solidity, then colours – blue and white. It drew up right by them, and a smiling man in a check suit, bow tie and reflector sunglasses got out.

'Team-leader Chen Runfa?'

Chen nodded imperceptibly.

'Ma Xueyi.' The man stuck out a hand. 'Supervisor, First Class, Customs Department. Welcome to the South!'

Chen grunted a reply. Ma opened a rear door and coolness poured out of the vehicle. As the visitors got in, they sank into the seats.

'Not this warm up in Beijing then?' said Ma.

Chen remained silent.

'You'll get used to it,' Ma went on. 'Take it easy for a couple of days.'

'We don't have time to take it easy,' Chen snapped. 'We've got work to do.' He took out a file and buried himself in it.

They passed the airport gates. Bao peered through the window at the greenery fountaining up by the roadside. In the capital, it cost the government to keep the dust-red city alive with parks and trees. Down here, the battle seemed to be to stop nature from running wild and devouring the streets and buildings. The thought came back to him, that this lead couldn't have been much further from Huashan had the criminals deliberately willed it to be.

'Can't you do something about this?' said Chen as the car tagged on to yet another traffic jam. 'Restrict vehicle usage or something? This is ridiculous!'

Ma shrugged. 'That's the way it is here. It's called prosperity.'

'It's anarchy. Put the siren on and get people to move out of our way! We're on state business!'

'No one would take any notice.'

'*Aiya,*' said Chen, and went back to his file.

*

The 747 began its approach, so low over the roofs of Kowloon that Zhao could see people in swimming pools and detect makes of car in the streets. Mercedes. Porsche. Jaguar. The Beijing policeman had done this journey many times in his imagination, now it was for real. The West!

The airliner touched down and the passengers disembarked along a tube into the glass and concrete maze called Kai Tak airport. There was a long queue at customs, but, as arranged, Zhao walked to the desk reserved for aircrew and VIPs, showed his badge and was waved through. In arrivals, he was confronted by a line of people with names on boards. A fantasy came into his mind, that a plump young girl would be waiting for him in a leather mini-skirt and black stockings. She would sweep him off in a Rolls Royce to her flat on the peak, pour out two glasses of champagne ...

A middle-aged Westerner with a drooping moustache was holding out a piece of cardboard with the character 'Zhao' in the old-style writing they still used down there. He stuck out a blotchy, red-haired hand. 'Donald Fish. Inspector, Royal Hong Kong Police.'

'Oh, er, Zhao. Zhao Heping. Pleased to meet you.'

Fish nearly smiled. 'Let me take your bag. You had a good journey?' he said, in good Cantonese.

'Yes. CAAC keep all their prettiest stewardesses for the international flights!'

Fish looked embarrassed and started for the terminal door. Outside, a car was waiting. In the back was an interpreter from Xinhua News Agency, China's unofficial embassy in Hong Kong.

'I'm Ming Aiguo,' the interpreter said. Zhao shook his hand coolly. There was no real need for Ming to be here. The Englishman's Cantonese was OK and his own was excellent. The car sped off down a freeway lined with bright adverts for smart clothes, designer shades and the latest electronic gadgets.

His host tried to be friendly. 'This is our tunnel,' he said, as the car disappeared into a tunnel.

Zhao nodded politely.

'This is Hong Kong Island,' said Fish, as the car re-emerged on Hong Kong Island.

Another nod.

'And this is Wanchai.'

Zhao's face lit up.

'A centre of decadence,' Interpreter Ming commented.

'What's that place?' Zhao asked, pointing at a doorway surrounded by pictures of half-naked women.

Fish grimaced. 'That's the Golden Lotus Club.'

'That is a place to be avoided,' said Ming.

'Is it expensive?' Zhao asked Fish jokily.

'Everything is expensive in Wanchai,' Fish replied. 'Except the trams.'

Zhao told himself he'd avoid the trams.

*

Supervisor Ma Xueyi's office was an airy, white-walled room with a window that opened on to a garden of explosive purple bougainvillea. An enormous propeller fan on the ceiling clanked round.

'We have no reason to suspect the smuggler was anything but a tourist,' Ma was saying. 'His name was Claude Bonnet, aged forty-five, from Paris, France – '

'I know where Paris is,' Chen cut in.

'Of course. Bonnet has no previous convictions. We checked with Interpol. He was part of a tour group, on its way back out to Hong Kong. He bought the Buddha from a pedlar, for five hundred yuan – '

'How much?' It was Bao's turn to interrupt.

'These tourists have money to burn.'

'No, no. Those things are worth thousands and thousands in the West.'

'I must question this smuggler at once,' said Chen.

Ma grinned with embarrassment. 'That, er, might be difficult.'

'Difficult?'

'He's gone home.'

'Home?'

'Yes. To Paris, Fr … '

'This man is a key witness in a major police inquiry. Where's your Unit Secretary? I want to speak to him at once.'

'We consulted top officials in Beijing,' Ma said nervously. 'They told us to avoid a diplomatic incident.'

'I don't believe you,' said Chen.

'I can show you the documents,' said Ma.

'They couldn't have let this man go. Knowing the seriousness of this investigation.'

Ma began rifling through his desk. He found the papers and handed them to Chen, who read them in silence.

'Secretary Wei signed this,' the team-leader finally said. 'And Minister Hu.' Then he went silent again. For a long while, there was only the noise of the fan and the traffic outside. A mosquito whined past Bao's ear, and he swatted it.

'Got to watch out for those buggers,' said Ma, forcing a smile on to his face.

Bao nodded. 'So, you know where Bonnet brought the item, then?'

'Of course.'

'What sort of place is it?'

'A street market.'

'One with regular stallholders?'

'Yes.'

'I think we should talk to these people. Don't you, Comrade Team-leader?'

Chen shook his head. 'You go,' he said, his voice a whisper, then returned to the papers.

Supervisor Ma jumped to his feet. 'I'll organize transport straight away!'

*

The Police motorbike nosed a path through the wall of shoppers and drew up at the kerb.

'That's the place,' said Ma. He got off the bike. Bao climbed out of the sidecar and was led to a stall festooned with dayglo nylon shirts.

'Kwok Man-ho,' he said, pointing at the owner. 'He saw Bonnet meet up with the vendor.'

Kwok grinned and began jabbering in Cantonese. Ma translated. 'He says he knew the guy was up to no good the moment he saw him.'

'What actually happened?' Bao asked. Witnesses often had this second sight, even when observing perfectly innocent people.

More Cantonese.

'He says the guy stood on the corner, waiting for foreigners. When Bonnet came past, he stopped him. They talked. They disappeared. That's it.'

'I'm sure that happens all the time in a big tourist city. Why report this to you?'

'We came round with a picture of Bonnet, asking if anyone had seen him. Several people had done. He had a pair of loud green trousers on.'

'Ah. Did this vendor talk to every foreigner?'

The stall-holder didn't know.

'And then you got a tip-off, am I right?' Bao asked the Cantonese officer.

'Yes. One of the hotel staff saw the Buddha in Bonnet's room. He could tell it was an antique, and reckoned the guy was going to try smuggling it out of the country.'

'Could I speak to this fellow?'

'The tip was anonymous.'

'Have you interviewed all the staff?'

Ma looked surprised. 'We have to respect informants' confidentiality.'

'I understand.' Bao paused. 'This has been most useful.' He turned to the stallholder. '*M–koi, Kwok Sin–shaang*,' he said: *thank you, Mr Kwok*, in his best Cantonese – which wasn't very good.

Kwok couldn't hide his amusement.

*

'Find anything?' said Chen when they got back.

Bao shook his head. 'Not really.'

'Didn't think you would. These petty businessman types are most unreliable. You're lucky they didn't try and sell you some shoddy piece of rubbish made in Hong Kong.'

Bao hid the kit-bag he had brought behind his chair.

'Meanwhile,' the team-leader went on, 'I've been doing some useful work. I have a list here of all the major hotels. In the next few days, we will visit them and ask every single foreign tourist if they have seen any other artefacts from Huashan on sale. Sets of photographs are being faxed down tonight. I suggest starting with the biggest establishments and working downwards. You deal with the White Swan; I'll take the Liuhua. Any objections?'

'No.'

'It will be a lot of work, and we will need to be alert the whole time. There is a distinct possibility that some of these foreign tourists might in fact be agents. I suggest we turn in early, in preparation.'

Their host looked disappointed. 'If you want to see the city by night, I could show you around. It's quite an experience. I know a great karaoke bar, with some nice girls – '

'We have work to do tomorrow, Comrade Ma.'

The local man glanced at Bao, who in turn looked at his frowning boss.

'Maybe another evening,' said the inspector.

*

The two Beijingers dined in the officers' canteen, at a table in a corner. Chen was silent the whole evening, except for a few disparaging comments about the cost of a banquet going on nearby: eleven senior policemen at a round table stacked high with food, getting louder and drunker as the evening went on.

Bao went to bed early, then lay awake, unable to sleep. The humidity! He got up and threw open the window. Noise came pouring in: car horns, bike bells, revving engines, music. He closed the window again, then realized he should never have opened it in the first place, as the room was now full of insects. So he lay sweating under the gauze cone of his mosquito net, while various creatures fluttered and rattled against it. Surely one would find a way through … When he finally drifted off to sleep, he dreamt. The usual dream this time: death at Muxudi.

*

Inspector Zhao dined with Interpreter Ming in one of the Xinhua accommodation blocks.

'I envy you, returning home so soon,' said Ming. 'This is a foreign country in so many ways.' He shook his head sadly. 'The agency does its best to make us feel at home, but it's not easy.'

Zhao helped himself to another square of pork gristle and tried to look sympathetic. Around the walls were pastel landscapes of the homeland in traditional style.

'I shall be lucky if I go back north before next Spring Festival,' Ming went on. 'There's nothing quite like Spring Festival in Zhengzhou, you know.'

'I'm sure.'

A tepid bowl of wonton soup followed, then a boiled sweet. Zhao pleaded tiredness.

'I think I'll have an early night.'

'Good idea. Don't forget – if you can't sleep, there's a television room where we can get CCTV.' Ming shook his head. 'The Hong Kong stuff is so vulgar.'

Back in his room, Zhao checked the place for bugs. There didn't seem to be any, but just in case, he set his clock radio to play for an hour. He slid the window open with concentrated caution.

A small ledge ran beneath each line of windows. A man of his skill and agility would have no problem edging along it as far as the vertical guttering. Then there was the outer wall, scanned by a closed-circuit camera mounted on the roof. The camera seemed fixed: it looked to have a regulation issue 35 mm lens, so there would be a large blindspot on the left.

Zhao retreated to take one last look in the mirror, smoothed back his hair, then climbed out into the hot tropical night.

Chapter Twelve

Inspector Zhao made his way down the dimly lit stairs of the Golden Lotus Club. A second bouncer at the foot asked him for more money.

'That was entrance up there. This is membership.'

Despite his linguistic abilities, Zhao found this distinction too subtle to understand. However, the one thing he mustn't do was to kick up a fuss.

'How much?'

'Fifty dollars.'

Zhao stifled a groan, produced the money then smiled at the thought of the journey back from Huashan, most of which he had spent persuading Chen how big a budget this Hong Kong mission would require.

By Western standards it was still early. The long chrome bar was deserted except for a dinner-jacketed barman cleaning glasses. Two girls in low-cut blouses, mini-skirts and black stockings stood in a corner, deep in conversation despite the synthesized disco music swirling around their ears.

Trying to look confident, Zhao walked over to the bar. One of the girls looked up and flicked a glance at him. Some kind of signal?

Don't rush.

The barman approached. 'Drink, sir?'

'I'll have a beer.'

'The wine list is here, sir. I can recommend the Dom Perignon '66.'

'Oh, thanks. I'll have a bottle –' He saw the price. '*Aiya!*' Zhao ran his finger up the price column till he found some stuff called Champagne Du Maison, which was only seventy-five dollars. He began taking out the cash.

'That's dollars US. It's four hundred HK.'

The sum transformed itself into *renminbi*, into weeks worked, months of savings, years of rent. Zhao grinned, then counted out the money and handed it over.

'A waitress will bring it to your table, sir.'

'Good.' Zhao walked off and sat down in a comfortable corner. A few minutes later, a girl in a *qipao* split to the top of her thigh came over with two glasses and a substantial part of Zhao's budget bobbing in a huge silver cooler.

'Will you join me?' said the inspector, reaching for the bottle. The waitress smiled – her lacquer lipstick stayed shiny and unbroken – shook her head and strutted away. Zhao watched her go, then slowly poured himself a glass and raised it to nobody in particular.

'*Ganbei!*'

'*Ganbei!*'

Zhao spun round. A woman had taken the seat next to him. She was in her late thirties, her eyes heavy with mascara, her cheeks rouged and puffy.

'I'm Lily,' she said. 'Lily Wong. D'you mind if I join you?' When she smiled, little lines snaked out from the corners of her lips.

Zhao was about to say yes, he did mind – but he caught sight of the barman with a smirk on his face.

'No,' he said instead. 'Please do.' He added an extravagant gesture of welcome as if Lily were exactly the companion he had been waiting for.

'Can I have a drink?' said Lily.

'Of course!' He poured one out. '*Ganbei!*' he said again.

'*Ganbei!*' The glasses clinked, and Zhao was suddenly overcome with pleasure. There was a glass of proper French champagne fizzing in his hand. Lily had put on delicious perfume, and was looking at him with deep brown eyes. An older woman would know more, understand more. The girls by the bar suddenly seemed shallow, jangling and cold.

'So, you're from – over there.'

'You can tell that easily?'

'Your accent.'

'Not the clothes?'

'No,' Lily lied. She reached over and scraped a speck of dandruff off Zhao's shoulder.

'Well, I'm over here now – and I want to enjoy myself.'

'You will. I'll make sure of that.'

*

Bao arrived at the White Swan Hotel early next morning. For a moment he stood and stared at the astounding display in the lobby – an enormous waterfall, plunging into a rockpool amid a mock jungle of exotic plants – then he disappeared into one of a line of soundproofed telephone booths. He dialled his office.

Lu answered. 'Hello, sir. It's nice to hear you. It's awfully boring here. How are things in Guangzhou? It must be nice to – '

'There's a number I want you to investigate. Find out who it belongs to, and everything you can about the subscriber. And don't let them know you're on to them. If in doubt, stay in the background. Understand? Background. Especially if it's a private number and they have a beautiful daughter.'

'Yes, sir.'

'The number is 632-1275. Got it?'

Lu read the number back.

'Good. Don't try and contact me here. Just get the information. I'll ask you for it when I see you.'

'Yes, sir.'

The phone began to make a series of bleeping noises and cut him off.

*

The interviews were done individually, Bao confronting the nervous tourists with the pictures and asking if they had seen any of the artefacts on sale. So far, out of seventy-three, none had.

'Next, please.'

A youngish overseas Chinese in chinos and a Lacoste T-shirt entered and announced himself as George P Lim. Bao ticked him off the list. The inspector uncovered the photographs.

'Wow!'

Bao smiled. At last, some kind of reaction.

'Tang Dynasty, they must be,' Lim went on in Mandarin. 'The Golden Age of Chinese Culture.'

Bao smiled even more.

'And they've been stolen?' Lim went on. 'Maybe if you guys spent less time shooting students and more time guarding property – '

Bao's smile vanished. 'I had nothing to do with the Tiananmen incident,' he snapped, though he was under strict instructions not to discuss politics.

'But you approve, I take it?' said Lim.

'I'd hardly say if I didn't, would I?'

'No. I guess not ...' Lim nodded and went back to the photos. 'That's one hell of a haul,' he said at the end. 'Where did they come from?'

Bao was also under instructions to keep things moving. But he was fed up with frightened, ignorant tourists and suddenly wanted to talk with this man. 'You really want to know?' he asked.

'I do,' said Lim. He took a wallet out of his jacket pocket, from which he produced a card. 'I'm in the same line of business as you. George P Lim, San Francisco Police Department.'

Bao shook the man's outstretched hand. He knew he should make an excuse and terminate this conversation, but something inside him rebelled. Maybe it was that southern influence. He began to tell the story.

*

Someone was knocking on the door. 'Is everything all right in there?'

George Lim scowled. 'Hell, that's Empress Wu. Our tour guide. Get on the wrong side of her, and she'll make your holiday hell. I'd better go. It's been nice talking with you, Zheng.' He offered his hand, gave Bao another pumping handshake, then headed for the door. As he grabbed the handle, he paused then turned round.

'Why don't you join Amy and me for dinner tonight?'

Bao looked shocked. 'I'm not sure if we're allowed – '

'If you want to do something badly enough, you do it. That's an American attitude. I recommend it. Seven o'clock, in the lobby.'

*

Constable Lu cursed. The rain was constant, and nobody had used the phone in the last half hour. But orders were orders.

He was watching one of those private phone bureaux. Senior Party members got telephones free of charge, but ordinary citizens had to pay several months' wages for them. To afford this luxury, many city dwellers had set themselves up as public phone boxes, and the most entrepreneurial ones become bureaux, making calls and taking messages for their customers. 632-1275 had turned out to be one such outfit. Lu was now keeping their premises under surveillance, disguised as one of the thousands of itinerant bike-repair men in the capital.

Another rivulet of water wriggled down his back. A man appeared, wheeling a Flying Pigeon whose chain had come loose. After a short haggle over the cost of the repair, Lu got to work. He was actually quite good at mending things, and was so engrossed in his task that he missed the customer walking into the bureau.

A note changed hands and a satisfied Beijinger pedalled off into the rain. Lu wiped his hands on a cloth, tried to light a cigarette, toyed with the money in his pocket – then the customer emerged from the bureau. Lu glanced up at him, and their eyes met. Lu looked away at once and started fiddling with a gear mechanism someone had left to be fixed. The man walked away.

'I know him,' Lu said to himself. How? Where?

He suddenly felt an overwhelming desire to follow him. But he'd been told to stay put. Orders are orders.

*

Bao Zheng found a bench under a palm tree and sat down. It was a lovely evening, warm and breezy. The Pearl River lapped by. Old folk in Mao suits stood swaying through routines of *taijiquan*. On the bench next to him, a young couple were kissing. In public!

All part of the increasing Western influence on China – in which Bao was about to participate, by dining with George and Amy Lim.

He felt the fear again. The West was the enemy. Historically it had bullied the old China into humiliation. This was continuing today, via the viciously unfair economic system, Capitalism, that it sought to impose all round the world. Culturally, a creeping amorality came with that system. Money alone set the rules. There was no concept of virtue, personal or public. There was no justice, just the crude, momentary judgement of the marketplace. The god of money bent and twisted humanity into whatever shape it required.

Have nothing to do with Western influences!

But had felt a real link with George, a fellow cop and also someone genuinely proud of his Chinese heritage. And he was curious. What *was* life like in the West? Really? Truthfully?

Distinguish between what is known and what is presumed.

He had not told Chen about this meeting. As he sat watching Guangzhou going about its business, he realized that another reason why he was doing this was that nobody would find out. He was not part of anything down here; nobody knew who he was, or cared. It was a strange feeling.

A clock struck seven.

'Damn. Now I'm late. What will they think of me?'

George and Amy Lim were waiting in the hotel lobby, looking at a glass case of ginseng products 'guaranteed to restore the male member to maximum power' and sharing a joke.

'Zheng, I want you to meet my wife.'

Amy Lim, also a second-generation refugee from Mao's China, held out a soft, smooth hand to the Communist Party member. Bao wasn't sure what to do. Should he kiss it, like westerners in old films sometimes did? He took hold of it and gave it a brief shake, and was rewarded by a charming smile.

'George has told me all about you,' she said.

Bao stammered a reply. The three visitors walked out into the delicious tropical evening.

'I want to eat snake tonight,' said George. 'I believe there's a marvellous restaurant in town that serves nothing else.' Amy screwed up her face. 'George!'

'Zheng, you like to eat snake, don't you?'

'I've never tried.'

'Really? Then it's an adventure for all of us.' He strode up to a taxi and shouted a command to the driver. 'By the way, everything's on me tonight,' he added as they got in. Bao shook his head, George insisted, Bao refused – the taxi left the island

and began to wind its way up the back alleys of the great southern city.

*

The Snake Restaurant was full of Chinese businessmen shouting into mobile phones and Western tourists giggling at the items on the menu. The new arrivals were shown to a private room where they could be charged extra. Bao noticed a microphone by the ventilator. George did, too, and took out some gum, chewed it for a moment then stuck it over the opening. Bao felt a childish thrill at this.

They had agreed to avoid politics, anyway. Instead, they shared stories. Work and family. The past: George's ancestors had come from round here, while Amy's were from Fujian, the next stop on their itinerary. After that, George said, they would be in Beijing.

Bao suddenly felt grown-up and gawky again. He wanted to be their host in the capital, but that could be difficult. Yet it would be undignified not to offer them hospitality of some kind.

'Where are you staying there?' he asked finally.

'The Kangxi Hotel. You know it?'

'Yes,' Bao replied. It was right next to the Qianlong, the hotel where Jasmine Ren had sung. His mood sank further, at the thought of the Xun Yaochang case.

George Lim was refilling their small Maotai glasses. He handed one to Bao.

'*Ganbei!*' said the American, and downed it in one.

Amy Lim did the same.

Bao raised his glass. '*Ganbei!*' The clear, powerful spirit seared down his throat.

Drink and sing. How long is life?

Chapter Thirteen

At the end of the week, Constable Lu didn't have much to report. Lots of faces, most of whom he'd forgotten; one or two regulars on whom he'd made notes. The man he thought he'd recognized – he still couldn't place him. Maybe he'd been wrong. He had also become better at mending bicycles, (easily) won a fight with another repair-man who reckoned Lu was trying to muscle in on his patch, and earned more than a police constable earned in a month. He had just fixed a puncture – another one yuan fifty – when he looked up and saw the man again.

Luckily it was only a side view, so there was no eye contact this time. The man didn't seem to notice Lu as he hurried into the bureau or as he left it, about fifteen minutes later and headed north.

'Now!' said the young constable. 'I have to!'

'No!' a voice inside told him, but he had already packed his tools into the pannier and was wheeling his bike down the *hutong*.

Remember what they taught you at Police College. Keep your distance. Merge in with the crowd.

Lu nearly lost him several times, but when he emerged on to Chongwen Street, there was his quarry, talking to a rickshaw driver. Haggling? The man got in, and the pedal-powered vehicle creaked off. Lu followed slowly up the rain-soaked bike lane, always extra careful, always pacing himself to look natural but never losing sight of the rickshaw. His quarry turned into Zhanxi, jinked past the International Hotel, and swung down on to the capital's new ring road.

The Kangxi Hotel came into view. Then the Qianlong. Lu stifled a cry of astonished excitement as the rickshaw turned into the second of the two driveways.

*

The plane from Guangzhou touched down at Beijing airport at about six-thirty. A car was at the airport to meet Chen.

'I'd offer you a lift, Bao Zheng, only it's not really in my direction,' said the team-leader. 'See you tomorrow morning.'

Bao was quite happy to take a bus. As it bumped back into town, he tried to get comfortable on the plastic seat, and gazed out at the thorn-trees and the dry, red earth. It might not be lush, but it was home.

Back at Flat 1008, he went straight to the kitchen and prepared himself a northern meal, one with a decent amount of spices and with noodles, not rice. He put on a cassette of Beijing Opera and sat sipping green tea on his little balcony looking out over the roofs of the capital.

The south was already a memory. A fascinating and beautiful one, but not where he belonged. He was a northerner, Shandong-born like Confucius and now part of the life of the capital. After his evening with the Lims, he'd never listen to some of the official talk about America with the same total belief again – though as he thought this, he realized how much less such stuff was around nowadays anyway. He felt a little more a citizen of the world – but he still belonged here, in the north of China.

He still wasn't quite sure how he would deal with George and Amy when they arrived in Beijing. He'd make it official this time. A chance to study police methods from other countries. 'Make the Foreign Serve China,' as Mao himself had said. And if it didn't work, George and Amy would understand.

He sat down and began some *qigong* exercises. Let those thoughts go, all of them. Just breathe. In, out …

R-ring!

He stifled a curse and walked over to the phone.

'Yes,' he snapped.

'Oh, hello, sir. It's Lu here.'

'What d'you want?'

'Could we meet?'

'Not again!'

'It's important.'

'OK. Same place?'

'Yes, please. In half an hour?'

*

As Lu told his story, Bao listened in silence. At the end, the inspector said nothing.

Lu looked worried. 'I did do the right thing, sir, didn't I?'

Bao glanced up. 'Yes. Of course.' He clapped the young lad on the shoulder.

'Thank you, sir.'

'We mustn't jump to conclusions, that's all. We don't know that the character you followed was anything to do with the Huashan thieves, simply that he used the same telephone bureau and ended up at that hotel.'

Lu nodded. 'But it's a coincidence, don't you agree?'

'Yes.'

'And you're always saying how you don't believe in coincidences.'

'Yes ...' Bao stared down at the ground, lost in thought. Then he straightened up. 'Lu, you mustn't mention any of this to anyone. Not to Team-leader Chen, not to Secretary Wei ... You've done well, extremely well. But now you must keep quiet. Totally quiet. *Disaster begins with an open mouth.*'

*

Bao pedalled slowly back to his flat from their meeting-place. He put his bike in the rack and locked it, summoned the lift, cursed – the lift shut off at nine-thirty – and walked slowly up the stairs. Back inside, he crossed to his writing desk, took out his notebook and sat down.

Everything about the case so far, however irrelevant it might seem.

Distinguish between what is actually known and what is presumed.

What are the 'pressure points' and what action should be applied there?

After this, he took a larger sheet of paper and drew a diagram. He placed the Qianlong Hotel at the centre. Radiating out from it were lines connecting to boxes filled with names, dates, events. In one corner he wrote Huashan. Then he linked that up to the hotel: a line from the Goddess of Mercy to the *Yi Guan Dao*? Why not? Of course! He paused to think, whirling his pencil round the back of his hand. Another line …

It was nearly midnight by the time he had produced a diagram that satisfied him. There were still gaps. One was the murder of Xun Yaochang, which fitted in some ways but not in others. Was he trying too hard to squeeze it in to the story?

He would find out.

*

Bao wrote a note to his mentor, Commissioner Da, explaining what he believed and the actions he would be taking in the light of that. Half way through, he felt a frisson of fear – did one ever truly know anyone else? Da had known about the raid on Ren Hui's house – and it was possible that someone senior was connected to the Huashan raids in some way. But you have to trust your judgement of people in the end.

Don't you?

He carried on writing.

*

The senior team reunited for the drive back to Huashan next

morning, Inspector Zhao told Team-leader Chen of all the work he had done in Hong Kong.

'I must have met every policeman and every informer in the colony,' he said. 'None of them knew anything.'

'You certainly spent enough money!' Chen commented.

Zhao shrugged. 'I said it was an expensive place. I was right. Nothing comes cheap, least of all information.'

'But we haven't got any information.'

'I think we can be certain that those artefacts aren't going through Hong Kong or Macao.'

'Then what the hell was that Buddha doing in Guangzhou?'

'I don't know,' Zhao replied, suddenly looking dejected.

'I think it was deliberate,' put in Bao. 'A diversion. Maybe there's probably a boatload of these things heading for Taiwan right now.'

'We certainly didn't find too much in Guangzhou,' said Chen. 'And I was appalled by the laxity of our colleagues down there, both ideologically and professionally. I got the distinct impression that Supervisor Ma Xueyi would do anything for money.' He paused. 'And yet much of our Revolution was created in the South. I can't help feeling that something has gone wrong down there. That whole part of the country has succumbed to what Chairman Mao referred to as sugar-coated bullets. Bourgeois comforts, cultural frivolity, foreign ideology.'

Chen carried on in a similar vein for a while, after which Bao's enthusiasm for sharing his own views about the Guangzhou Buddha waned. Nobody seemed to mind his reticence, which suited him fine.

A few more miles, and the car turned off metalled road on to the track that led up the Huashan valley, first through a pine forest, then across open rock. They reached the compound gates. Constable Tang, promoted to driver for the day, hooted the horn until somebody came to let them in.

*

Bao sat in Cave One, panting like an old man.

'You shouldn't have attempted the climb in your condition at this time of day,' said Fen, now formally appointed Chief Security Officer. 'I'm not having medical emergencies up here.'

'I'm not a "medical emergency",' Bao replied irritably.

'I'm tightening up all round,' Fen went on. 'Safety and security. I'm determined to catch this thief.'

'So am I,' said Bao. He waited till his pulse was nearly normal, then left the cave. He walked slowly up the path, making a short detour into Cave Twenty-two to look at the wall paintings. At the top of the site, he found two guards playing *xiangqi* chess. Despite Fen's talk of tightening up, they let him pass without demur.

It did not take long to reach the point from which Wu had fallen. Bao stood staring down at the cracked lip of the path.

Time to test a part of his hypothesis. He lay face-down on the pathway, spreading his weight as evenly as possible, reached over the side of the ledge, and began groping around. He soon found a crevice. He had to wriggle closer to the edge of the path to really feel inside it – the image of Wu's body flashed into his mind as he did so. There was nothing. Then his fingers brushed something hard and shiny. Then that 'something' moved. A scorpion emerged from the crevice and skittered across the rock face. Bao wondered if the same thing hadn't happened to Wu. He paused – did the creature have a partner? – then resumed his search.

And then he found it: smooth, flat and round. He pulled gently at it, and it came easily.

'Careful!' he told himself. The memory of smashing Meng Lipiao's fake ceramics came back to him. But this piece was real. Soon after he was sitting on the pathway looking at a stoneware plate with a rich bottle-green glaze. It wasn't in the class of the missing Guanyin, but it was a genuine antiquity, stolen from the caves and hidden up here.

He was on the right track at last.

Chapter Fourteen

Bao sat and ate the meal he had brought along. When he had finished, he threw the chicken bones and orange peel out over the precipice and watched them curl away into the valley below. Then he wrapped the stolen plate in the now-empty food-bags and stuffed it in his pack.

He took his time on the way down. He joined in the chess game with guards by the outcrop, made a necessary visit to the latrine, and wandered into Cave Twenty-two to admire the paintings again. He was just passing Cave One, when the new security officer, Fen, appeared.

'Comrade Bao, a moment, if you please. We're carrying out random searches of personnel.'

'Very wise,' said Bao.

Fen took the inspector's day-pack and began checking the contents. 'Liao, make a note of these. Flask, one, empty. Notebook, one. Pen, one.' Fen turned the pack upside down, shook it, crumpled it, then handed it back. Meanwhile, another constable ran his hands over the detective's body, checking pockets, his holster, even his trouser turn-ups.

'Your men are thorough,' Bao commented. 'I congratulate you.'

'Thank you,' said Fen curtly. 'You may proceed.'

Bao carried on down the mountain.

*

Late in the afternoon, the site latrines were emptied. Bao watched as a a vat of excrement was lowered down the hoist and carried by the most junior porters to a cesspit, where it would be emptied, swabbed out and left to dry in the hot summer sun.

The pit was some way from the camp, and hidden from it by a ridge of rock and a copse of pine trees.

'Quite right, too,' Bao said to himself as he crossed the ridge and was hit by the stench.

He thought of the millions of night-soil collectors who spread this stuff on the fields day in, day out. Shit-shovellers: that sergeant put it so well. Country-born CSO Wu would have known the reality of that.

He took a stick, and, fighting back rising nausea, began poking around in the cesspit. It did not take him long to find the plate, still wrapped in those plastic lunch-bags. He hauled it out and gave it a very thorough slooshing from the hose that was kept there to clean the vat. He took a pair of tongs from his pocket and removed the plate from its protective coats. It was undamaged, untarnished and safely off the mountain. Finally, he took the plastic away and buried it by the trees, returning to his office with the plate under his jacket.

The next task, of course, was to get it to Beijing.

After some thought, Bao hid the plate carefully in the VW Shanghai. In the past, the vehicle had never been checked on leaving the site, but with the new security officer in charge, he had to be more careful. He needn't have bothered, however: they were simply waved past.

No doubt all other senior officials' vehicles received the same treatment, Bao reminded himself.

*

It was a perfect summer weekend evening in Temple of Heaven Park. Golden sun filtered through the cypress trees. Gentle music wafted out of the park loudspeakers. Kites bobbed in a clear blue sky. An old man in a Mao suit sat playing folk tunes on an *erhu*.

The dust and paranoia of Huashan seemed a million miles away. Bao Zheng walked slowly along the pathway till he found a bench with a view of the Qinian Hall, the most beautiful building in China and thus, obviously, in the world. He sat and stared at its three azure roofs rocketing up into the sky. Perfection.

'Zheng!'

George Lim was alone and on time.

'George! Good to see you. Did you enjoy Fujian? And Suzhou?'

'Fujian was Amy's treat. Suzhou did it for me. Those gardens! That's what being Chinese is all about. Retirement to a world of classical beauty, to drink wine and read the classics in a moonlit, waterside pavilion.'

'That's the dream,' Bao agreed. He smiled at his American counterpart, then let his look turn more earnest. 'I need your help.'

'With the case?'

'Yes.'

'I don't want any trouble.'

'There won't be – for you. It's quite simple … '

*

George Lim walked into the gift shop of the Qianlong Hotel and browsed around. The assistant took no notice, only looking up from his martial arts magazine when Lim addressed him directly.

'Have you got anything better?' the American asked, pointing to the pottery section.

The young man shook his head.

'I'm looking for sculpture,' Lim went on. 'Really nice stuff. I'm prepared to pay,' he added, slapping two fifty-yuan Foreign Exchange Certificates on to the table.

The boy put his magazine down and made a grab for the notes. Lim snatched them back.

'I want the best. I'll be discreet.'

The boy looked him up and down. No, he wasn't a government agent. Nobody from the People's Republic could wear quite such expensive clothes in quite such a slapdash way, not even a cadre's son.

'Give me the money,' he said, 'and I'll introduce you to someone who'll sell you what you want.'

Lim held out one of the notes. 'You get the rest on satisfactory completion of purchase.'

'Be back here in an hour.'

*

Lim did as he was told, to the minute. He was greeted with a smile from a small fat man in a Western suit.

'If you'd like to come this way, sir.' The man led the way down a corridor and into an office. He offered George a padded leather chair and sat down at a desk. A third person sat watching the proceedings, his chin buried in his hands, a stupid malevolence in his eyes. Lim knew the type: minders for gangland big-shots.

'I want good art,' Lim began. 'And I want it old. Tang Dynasty, if possible.'

The small man nodded. 'You are, of course, aware that there is an export prohibition on any item more than a hundred years old.'

'I know. A guy was busted for it when I was down in Guangzhou.' Lim paused, then continued, 'I'm prepared to run the risk. The Tang is the golden era for me. Of art, of poetry, of sculpture. You only have one life, so why not have the best?'

'Very true. But what makes you think you can get items of that quality here? You're not on our hotel register.'

Lim shrugged. 'I'm staying at the Kangxi. They didn't have anything I liked.'

The man smiled. He knew Lim was telling the truth; he'd checked with his opposite number at the neighbouring hotel. He stood up, walked across to a drawer and took out several pieces of Sancai pottery, a vase, and a silver plate.

'How much is the warrior?' Lim asked.

'Twenty thousand.'

'Yuan?'

The man scowled. 'Dollars, US. If you want quality, you have to pay for it.'

'Yes, but ... '

The man packed all the goods away. A second, lower drawer contained inferior works. 'What about that?' Lim asked, pointing to a bronze of a galloping horse.

The vendor looked at his client with contempt. 'It's two thousand. You want to examine it?'

'Yes, please.'

Lim took it and held it. It was beautiful. It was also a fake, but still several centuries old and the work of a craftsman: antique collecting had become popular as early as the Ming Dynasty, so forgery had, too. This was as near as an honest sergeant in the SFPD was likely to get to owning a genuine Tang Dynasty artefact.

'Seven fifty,' he said.

The negotiations began.

*

Back in his room, Lim put the horse on his dressing table and stared at it. Western artists had had to wait for photography before they understood the mechanics of the gallop. His ancestors had known two thousand years earlier. Then he put it in the room safe and changed the combination.

At a quarter to four, he set out for the city centre. As he walked out of the front door, he spotted the man following him at once. He took a taxi to the Forbidden City; a second taxi followed. He joined the foreigners' queue; the tail tried to join him and was shunted on to the queue for mainland Chinese by a steward.

'I'll pay the extra!' the tail protested, but the official was adamant. The tail had come up against that most priceless of pearls, an honest official.

Lim didn't even look back as he headed down the long tunnel into the great Imperial Palace. He then fought back his natural fascination – he'd come back tomorrow with Amy – and walked briskly past the centuries of history on show. Leaving by the northern exit, he headed for the address Zheng had given him.

He knocked on the grimy wooden door, and an old woman led him through a rubbish-filled courtyard into a neat living room, where a group of people were sitting on a sofa. It was another of these private telephone bureaux, but one that Bao knew and trusted.

'Do you want a mug of tea?' asked the woman.

'Oh, thank you.'

'That'll be twenty fen.'

The other customers, alerted by his clothes and his accent, crowded round him. 'Are you American?' was their first question. When Lim said yes, they began bombarding him with queries about life in the States. When the current caller finished, they insisted he go next so they could all listen to his conversation.

'Please, this is private,' he protested. The woman began giving Lim's audience a lecture on politeness to foreign friends and shooed them away. The American dialled and got through.

'Hello, Zheng? Good ... Yes, I did everything you wanted.'

'Thank you. So – what did the fellow look like?'

'Short, fat, Western suit. Rings on his fingers. In his thirties, I'd guess.'

Bao looked through the dossier of photographs he had been preparing all day. 'Square sort of chin?'

'Yeah.'

'Puffy eyes?'

'That's the guy. I didn't get a name, I'm afraid.'

'That's OK. He's called Li Dehong. What were the pieces on offer like?'

'Lovely. He knows his trade. But there was nothing there from the list you gave me.'

'No, there wouldn't be. Those would be extra, extra special, for export only. I hope you got yourself something nice.'

'I did.'

'Ma Xueyi will look after you. Any reaction from Li when you mentioned Guangzhou?'

'No.'

'Ah. Never mind.'

'He's a cool customer.'

'Yes ... Tell me about the room: access, contents, lay-out.'

Lim did so.

'And was Li alone?'

'No. He had a bodyguard. A guy who just sat in the corner, watching. Big, mean-looking.'

'Any distinguishing marks?'

Lim thought of the man, sitting and staring. 'Didn't see any.'

'Were you followed?'

'Yes.'

'I'm sorry about that. They may keep an eye on you for another day or so, till they get bored with all the tourist sites. I'm afraid it means we can't really meet up.'

'I guessed that. You'll just have to come to the USA instead.'

'Yes ...' Bao replied. The idea, which would have been anathema even a few days ago, suddenly seemed attractive. 'Anything else worth mentioning?'

'Don't think so.'

'Thanks for everything, George. You've done me a huge favour. And your home country.'

'My home country is America, Zheng. But I know what you mean.'

Bao sent his best wishes to Amy. The two policemen said their goodbyes, then the conversation was over.

It was best that way.

*

That evening, Bao took his diagram out of the false bottomed drawer where he had concealed it, scrubbed out a dotted line and replaced it with a clear, strong one.

Chapter Fifteen

The door of the cell creaked open. Jasmine Ren glanced up from the corner where she now spent most of the day in a silent huddle. Instead of leaping to her feet and attacking the new arrival, she just turned her head and muttered: 'Oh, it's you.'

The warder pulled up the cell's one chair for the visitor to sit on. Bao ignored him and squatted down on the floor.

'Leave us, please, warder. And close the shutter and turn off the intercom.'

'Sir, I think – '

'Do as I say.'

The warder gave a shrug and went out.

'Trying to be nice?' said Jasmine. 'Trying to win me over with a little display of trust? Or have you got something nastier in mind? I wouldn't put it past you dogs – '

'I want to talk in private, that's all.'

'I've got nothing new to say. How many more times do I have to say it? I stuck that knife in Xun Yaochang's neck.'

Bao leant forward. 'Show me where, exactly.'

'D'you really want me to?'

'Yes. Why not?' Bao stretched forward a bit more. 'The precise spot, please.'

Jasmine paused then jabbed her finger into Bao's neck. The inspector winced.

'I'm glad that hurt,' she said.

'It didn't,' he lied. 'And it wasn't anywhere near where Xun was stabbed.' That was the truth. 'I think it's time you retracted that fake confession of yours and told me the truth. Let's start – '

'Go to hell! I've said I did it. What more d'you want? I hated the cheating bastard. He deserved it. And I'm not playing any more of your silly games – '

'I can get your father released.'

Jasmine Ren fell silent.

'He's been kidnapped, hasn't he?' Bao went on. 'By the people stealing those statues.'

'I don't know anything about statues,' Jasmine said slowly.

Bao paused. 'If you want to help him, you must help me. I imagine the kidnappers have said that they'll kill him if you drop your story. They have told you that you must play along, even go to jail. They say they'll pay the right bribes and get you out when it's all clear.'

Jasmine tried to keep an expressionless face.

'You've got to understand quite how ruthless these people are,' Bao continued. 'I suspect you've been brought up with some notion that thieves are honourable. And they are, up to a point, until the sums of money are big enough or the police get too close. There's no guarantee that they'll keep their side of the bargain. None at all. They are more likely to kill your father and let you face a bullet. Much more likely. D'you see that?'

'How d'you know all this?'

'It's my business to know things.'

'Which is why you came snooping round our home setting up some phoney business deal.'

'That was a routine investigation. When we get your father released, you'll be glad we undertook it.'

'And how do I know you're not at it again? More lies, more deception – '

'You don't know. You have to choose to trust me.'

The singer stared at Bao for what seemed like an eternity. 'Why are you doing this? What's in it for you?'

'You're accused of a crime you didn't commit,' said Bao. 'I happen to believe in justice.'

Jasmine burst out laughing. 'Of course! So you joined the bloody police!'

'Exactly.'

She fell silent again.

'This is the only way you can save yourself,' Bao went on. 'And your father.'

More silence. 'What do you want me to do?' she said finally.

'Talk to me. Be honest.'

Jasmine looked round at the walls of the cell. 'What d'you want to know?'

'First, tell me about the Qianlong Hotel.'

'The Qianlong?'

'Yes. Tell me how you got the job there.'

The look of puzzlement on her face had to be genuine. 'Dad told me the job was going. A friend of his ran that side of things. I went and did a kind of test, and got the gig.'

'Who was this friend?'

'Mr Li. Is he involved in all this?'

'Possibly.'

'I'll kill him if he is.'

'You'll need to be out of prison to do that. And I'd let us deal with Mr Li if he is involved in criminal activities. You'll have a happier life. Can you tell me anything more about this Li?'

'Not really. He was a cold fish, but he never behaved disrespectfully. Looking back I never quite trusted him. But it's easy to say that, isn't it?'

'We don't have enough facts to judge him yet,' Bao said. '*Distinguish between what is known and what is presumed.* My motto.'

Jasmine stared down at the ground.

'Anyone else at the hotel I should know about?' Bao asked. 'Tell me about Chao.'

'Him,' Jasmine said with a scowl. 'He just hung around a lot. Sometimes I thought he fancied me, but I don't think he did. I never really worked out what he was there for.'

'And what about Zhang Kangmei? Eddie?'

'Poor old Eddie. He was head over heels in love with me. I can't say I felt the same. He's a melon. He should find another dreamer.'

'Does the name Luo mean anything to you? Or Pang?'

Jasmine looked puzzled. 'Luo Pang is a business colleague of my dad's. I don't think he's got anything to do with the Qianlong.'

'Tell me about him.'

'I don't know anything. It's just a name I've heard. He's important, I know that.'

'How?'

'Dad always said: "If Luo Pang calls, interrupt me, whatever I'm doing." But he never has called, not while I've been around, anyway. Is he part of this, too?'

'No. Maybe. I'm not even sure he exists.'

'He exists all right. I remember names.'

Bao offered Jasmine a Panda. The last one in the packet. 'Can we talk a bit about Xun Yaochang?'

'Do we have to?'

'Sorry, yes. The obvious question first: do you have any idea who did kill him?'

'No. He said there were guys after him. He said he had information about them, and was going to get money for it.'

'This was just before his death, right?'

'Yes. My dad forbade us to get together. I … had to accept that. But a couple of months later we got in touch again. He was a special guy, Officer. Totally different to most of the dickbrains father had working for him. He'd have gone far if ... '

She broke off. Bao nodded his head sympathetically.

'Do you think it was my fault?' she said after a long pause. 'Was it dad's doing. Carrying out his threat?'

'I don't know,' Bao replied. 'It's part of what I'm trying to find out.' He paused. 'Do you have any idea who he might have been going to the opera to meet the night he was killed?'

Jasmine shook her head. 'I wish I did.'

Bao pulled an envelope out of his pocket. 'Now I want you to look at some photographs. If you recognize any of them, tell me. And if possible, when and where you have met them.'

He laid a series of mug shots on the floor of the cell. One by one, everyone who worked at Huashan. Even his own colleagues.

'Remember, both your father's life and your own are threatened by people he regarded as friends. Neither you nor he owe a scrap of loyalty to any of them.'

'I see that.' Jasmine ran her eyes over the gallery of faces.

'That's your pal, isn't it? The young lad who came to one of my shows.'

'Quite right. You'd not seen him before, I take it.'

'Only when he came snooping round my father's. With you.'

'Anyone else you know?'

Jasmine shook her head. 'Sorry.' Then she pointed at a picture of Team-leader Chen, looking particularly owl-like in his heavy glasses. 'Who's that one?'

Bao felt a shiver of excitement. 'Why d'you ask?'

'He's ugly.'

'But you don't know him?'

'No. Never seen him before. Or any other of these people, apart from your young colleague. He's quite nice-looking, isn't he?'

'I suppose he has a youthful charm.'

'But he's a bit dim, I guess,' Jasmine said with a laugh.

Bao let the pictures lie there a while – how dare you accuse us, they seemed to say. Then he gathered them up and packed them away.

'Now, if I'm to help you, Jasmine, you'll have to carry on your act. You've confessed; our talk was a waste of time – '

The young singer's face lost its new-found sparkle at once. 'I can't go on for ever. D'you know what it's like, waiting to die?'

'Yes. One day I'll tell you about it, if you're interested in old soldiers' stories. Right now, you must have courage. And trust.' He looked her straight in the face.

'Trust … ' she replied hesitantly.

'One last thing,' Bao went on. 'If you hear that I have been killed, you must stop the act at once. Ask to speak to this man.' He was about to write down Commissioner Da's name, then gave Chai's instead.

'What about my father?'

'His kidnappers won't stick to any bargain. You'll be more help to him outside than in here.'

'Tell me who they are!'

'I can't.'

'If I'm supposed to trust you – '

'I don't know who they are,' Bao replied. 'Not for certain. When I do know for certain, I shall do whatever needs to be done.'

*

Bao returned to his office and sat at his desk, shuffling the photographs like a pack of cards. He laid them out on the table.

Dr Jian.

Professor Qiao.

Hei Shou, the Party man.

His own team; Chen, Zhao and Fang. The thought of treachery in his own team filled him with particular horror.

A supporting cast: Wu's deputy, Fen; the hoist operator, Zhang …

Even his mentor, Da, who had known about the raid on Ren Hui's house. (*all the facts, however irrelevant…*)

There was only one way to be certain.

He sat back in his chair. Yes, that would work nicely. First, he had to –

Someone was knocking at the door.

'Come in!' Bao's voice was cheerful, eager, alive.

Team-leader Chen entered. 'Are you ready, Comrade?'

'Ready? What for?'

'Political Study, of course. You didn't forget, did you?'

'Oh, no. Of course not.'

'It's going to be an old-fashioned Struggle Session. The Unit Committee will be looking at our self-criticisms again. With great thoroughness,' Chen added with a smugness born of knowing that other people's self-criticisms would be looked at with a lot more thoroughness than his own.

Bao Zheng's, for example.

*

The meeting was held in the Central Lecture Theatre. The Unit Committee – Secretary Wei, Colonel Yue from Internal Security and someone called Chu from the Technical Department – sat behind a long table on the stage. In front of it was a bare wooden chair, then banked rows of seats filled with *Xing Zhen Ke* staff.

Secretary Wei stood up and began to speak. He had a thin, scrawny face and a beak-like nose, almost as big as a Westerner's, that had earned him that nickname, Hawk.

'May and June 1989. Turbulent times. Times during which our loyalty and common sense were put under considerable pressure. But times from which we can all learn – if we are prepared to. We have all submitted self-criticisms, and they will all be reviewed in the coming months. I want to start today with one of particular interest. Will Detective Inspector (Second Class) Bao Zheng please step forward.'

Bao tried to keep the scowl off his face. He hadn't totally forgotten about 'Strengthen the Party', but he had put it to the back of his mind. It would all be OK. This stuff happened, and he had a measure of protection from Lao Da – unless, of course, the old man was connected to Huashan in some way. It would be unpleasant, that was all. He got to his feet and walked to the front of the room, with what he thought was the right level of confidence: no fear, of course, but not arrogance, either.

'Comrade Bao has recently concluded a murder investigation with great aplomb,' Wei said, forcing a grin on to his lips.

Bao grinned back. Was he actually going to get some praise?

'This makes the submission I have here all the more disappointing.' the Hawk went on, holding up Bao's self-criticism. 'Did you really think you could fool us with this?'

'I'm not sure what you mean, Comrade.'

'Yes you are. It was late, but that is excusable. What is not excusable is its content. Or lack of it. This submission is nowhere near full nor frank enough.' Wei began leafing through the pages. Colonel Yue stood up and whispered something in his ear.

They were going to bring up that business with the gun. A triviality. Let them.

'I have it on the best authority that you accepted a flower from one of the counter-revolutionaries,' Wei said instead. Bao's spirits fell. 'A flower. Is that true, Comrade Bao?'

'Well, I – '

'Is it true?'

'Yes. I can't see – '

'There's no mention of it here.'

'No.'

'Why?'

'It didn't seem significant.'

'You are an intelligent man.'

Bao tried to swallow but his throat had gone dry.

'You'd better tell us all about the incident now, Comrade.'

'Yes. Of course.'

He would have to grovel, admit that he had made a grave error, and beg for understanding. For a moment, a voice inside him protested. But he knew he had to override it.

'At that time, I did not realize the true nature of the counter-revolutionary uprising,' he began.

The Hawk listened in satisfied silence. When Bao had finished, he nodded his head, then opened the self-criticism again.

'There is also the extraordinary matter of the campfires. Apparently, Comrade Bao, you allowed a group of students to light a campfire, in deliberate contradiction of orders on the subject. I see no mention of this.'

'No. I've – been busy.' (He nearly added 'solving a murder', but that would have veered on the side of arrogance.) 'It got left out.'

'Tell us about it now, then.'

Bao began to mumble a second admission. The truth seemed to be shouting into his ear. The students had been almost children; their fires had reminded him of pioneers at camp, not dangerous counter-revolutionaries. He swallowed the truth and began a second apology.

Wei listened with a scowl on his face. Next, no doubt, would come the note Bao had sent to his superior. But instead, once Bao had finished, the Hawk went into a huddled discussion with his colleagues then got up to deliver judgement.

'I feel Comrade Bao could have spoken with more enthusiasm. We shall be watching him carefully in the next few months. But he does seem to have learnt a lesson. I would remind everyone here that ideological correctness is still the most important part of police work. Superficial concentration on expertise, without due thought for the aims to which expertise is directed, is of little value. Is that message clear, Comrade Bao?'

'Yes, Comrade Secretary.' Bao lowered his head.

A smile flickered across Wei's face. Then he turned to the assembled group of policemen and asked: 'Has anyone any comments to make?'

The ordeal was over. All Bao needed to do now was fill in a form, and he would be provisionally reinstated as a Party member and allowed to get on with his life. He began to rise from his chair.

'Comrade Secretary!'

The voice came from the back of the hall. A man was on his feet. Everyone turned to see who it was. It was Constable Hong, a former Red Guard now notorious for informing on his colleagues.

'I feel obliged to add a comment, Comrade Secretary,' Hong went on. 'Your information is incomplete. During the period under discussion, Comrade Bao also attempted to prevent members of the People's Liberation Army from carrying out their duties.'

Bao felt a wrench of fear in his stomach.

'Is this true?' Wei asked.

'I don't know what this man is talking about.'

'I was at Muxudi,' Hong went on, 'when PLA units met resistance from armed rioters. I distinctly heard Comrade Bao call out to them. He tried to tell the soldiers that the rioters weren't armed. He tried to tell the soldiers to stop defending themselves.' Hong paused. 'I hate to make such accusation about a fellow policeman, but given the delicacy of the current political – '

Secretary Wei cut him off with a wave of his hand. 'Comrade Bao, is this true?'

Bao opened his mouth, but no words came out.

'I've got witnesses,' said Hong.

'Let the Comrade Inspector answer!'

Still no words.

'Comrade Bao … '

Bao glanced across at Team-leader Chen, who was staring open-mouthed. Sergeant Fang was suddenly very busy polishing his glasses. Inspector Zhao was gazing into space. Lu was hiding behind a memorandum.

The inspector felt his fear redouble – then suddenly it was gone. He turned to Party Secretary Wei and looked him straight in the eye. 'Are you taking this man's word against mine, Comrade Wei?'

The Hawk looked shocked. 'Comrade Hong has provided useful information in the past.'

'He's a drunkard and a slacker. And now a liar.' Bao pointed a finger at Hong and followed it with a glare. 'I don't remember seeing you at Muxudi,' Bao told him, then turned back to the Secretary. 'For the moment I withdraw my application to rejoin the Party. I shall prove my case. I need time.'

'An honest admission now would be much better,' Wei replied. 'This legalistic rubbish wastes time.'

'Maybe. But that is my choice.'

'Very well. I think you will find it one that leads you into difficulty. The Party values spontaneous honesty, not the calculated half-truths of intellectuals.'

'I'm sure what the Party values above all else is truth.' Bao stepped down from the podium and returned to his seat amid a murmur of voices.

Chapter Sixteen

'You let your anger get the better of you,' Bao said to himself (how nice it would be to have someone to talk it all over with!)

No. This had been a trap. A confession would have led to real trouble. Question, was the trap caused by the Wei's simple enjoyment of bullying and by Hong's envy and spite, or were there deeper forces at work? Did someone want him out the way because he was in danger of exposing a criminal operation from which they took benefit?

He should play safe, abandon his plan, and revert to mindlessly filling in forms and asking routine questions at pointless interviews, until the Huashan operation was cancelled amid a fanfare of face-saving pronouncements about how hard everyone had struggled.

He lit another Panda.

It was dishonourable. And was it even 'safe'? Didn't the best safety lie in taking the offensive, in unmasking the thief?

*

It had been their secret: him and Peng Laolao, Granny Peng. The old woman had spent many afternoons filling the head of her bright, inquisitive second grandson with Chinese folklore. Bao had learnt geomancy, Daoism, legends – and the *Yi Jing*. But don't tell father. He won't approve.

He could see her now, unwrapping the yellowing text as she explained in a quiet voice how The Ancients had understood the nature of fate. 'Yin and Yang are always changing in Heaven,' she would say, taking down the paraphernalia of divination and laying it out on the table. 'Human affairs simply follow them.' She would bow, light the incense, mumble a prayer, and begin dividing the sticks.

A half-conscious glance round, a firm pulling-to of the curtains, and he walked over to his bookshelf. His fingers ran along the top to a dusty cardboard box and what looked like a bolt of material, then he lifted the items carefully down and placed them on his writing table. Inside the material was a book; the box contained three antique coins, two small incense jars and some incense-sticks. He put a stick in each jar and laid the book between them, facing due south. The coins went beside it. He lit the sticks.

His grandmother had kowtowed to the book, kneeling before it and tapping her forehead on the floor. Bao didn't feel it was necessary to do that, but gave a little bow anyway. The smoke from the incense-sticks began to spiral a clear, grey path to the ceiling.

'Our Ancestors will smell it, and know we are in need of guidance,' Laolao would say.

Bao muttered to himself that it didn't matter if a cat was black or white, as long as it caught mice.

Then it was time for the divination, the creation of two 'trigrams', six lines each yin or yang, the whole ending up as one of sixty-four possible outcomes, each one of which had been given meaning thousands of years ago. This should have been done with Peng Laolao's yarrow stalks (yarrow because it grew on the grave of Confucius), but they had long disappeared. Bao had bought some coins instead, from the reign of the Jiaqing Emperor (the last of those rulers to have been of any credit to his nation) and used them.

As with zen-style calligraphy, the art of using the *yijing* lay in getting into a calm mindset first, then acting promptly and clearly, without mental noise. Still the breath, concentrate on the issue at stake – the facts, not one's own emotions. When you know you are ready, begin.

Bao soon had the three coins, with their hollow square

centres, looking up at him from where he had lain them on the cloth having tossed them. Two tails and one head: a 'young' Yang line at the base of the lower trigram, a solid, unmoving call to action.

Bao had a sense, even then, how this would turn out. Two more lines, Yin this time, produced the bottom trigram, thunder, with no moving lines, so especially unambiguous. The pattern began to repeat itself – another Yang, another Yin... Bao prepared himself for the last line.

'Our Ancestors hear our unspoken words,' Laolao would say. Who heard now, in 1991?

He flipped the coins the final time. Head. Tail.

Head. A second thunder trigram, making hexagram number fifty-one. Bao didn't need to look it up. It was *Zhen*, double thunder. Explosive action. Attack leads to victory; waiting for the enemy's next move is fatal.

Bao doused the sticks, dismantled the set-up and put the pieces carefully back in their box. The book he wrapped back in its cloth, and everything went back to its hidden high place.

'I was going to do that anyway,' he told himself. But he still glanced at the old family photograph on the dresser and felt a deep, almost frightening gratitude welling up inside him.

*

'Here comes another one,' muttered the gatekeeper at the Qianlong Hotel. 'Hey, you!'

The new arrival, who was hunched over his coat as if hiding something beneath it, grinned. 'I've come to see Mr Li.'

'With an appointment?'

'No, but I – '

'Piss off!'

A ten-yuan note slapped down on to the window ledge.

The gateman pocketed the money. 'What's your business?'

'My business.'

'You won't get past the front door.'

Another note.

'Use the service entrance round the back.'

The man started up the hotel drive. Fifty or so yards short of the hotel steps, he cut across the lawn towards a large hole in the ground that was, according to a sign, going to become a 'Luxury Olympic-Size Swimming Pool'. A couple of workmen stopped to watch him go by, but said nothing. Bao Zheng reckoned that they had already learnt to keep quiet about the comings and goings here.

Round the back, was a huge loading bay. A man in a brown jacket was heaving sacks of rice off a truck. Bao made as if to speak to him, then a security guard appeared.

'I want to see Mr Li,' Bao told him.

The guard stared back. 'He hasn't got time for the likes of you.'

Ten more yuan.

'Wait here.'

The guard went off, and the man sat down on a tea-chest, lit a Panda cigarette then frowned.

'I should have taken a brand more in character,' he muttered, then took a drag. Bao was a perfectionist when it came to undercover work.

The guard took a while to return, anyway, by which time Bao had finished the Panda and got rid of the stub. The guard now had a tall man with him, who asked Bao in a thick Beijing accent what he wanted.

'To see Li Dehong. I have something for him.'

The tall man looked at him with a sneer.

'From Luo Pang,' Bao added.

The sneer vanished. 'You'd better follow me.'

He led Bao off through a fire door. A lock clicked ominously shut behind them; they climbed a flight of dingy steps and entered a dusty, stone-floored corridor.

'Wait here.'

The tall man's footsteps died away. Bao scanned the terrain with a soldier's eye. There were only exits at either end, plus a trapdoor in the ceiling which mightn't open anyway. No makeshift weapons to hand – but he didn't want a fight in his current condition anyway. He felt a momentary fear, then took control again.

Still, it was a long wait, especially as he couldn't have another Panda. But then the footsteps were back. Two sets, both different from those of the guard. Bao looked up at the new arrivals.

Bao suppressed a gasp. Li was one of them, but the other was Chao. A month or so ago he had stood, in police uniform, a few feet from this man. Now they were face-to-face again. Why hadn't George Lim said anything about the scar on Chao's chin?

For a second, that fear came back. Was Lim was part of the conspiracy, too? Had their meeting in Guangzhou been set up?

He took a deep breath and forced a smile onto his face. Li probably had more than one minder. Or maybe Lim had made a mistake: no wonder there was so much crime in America. 'Can we talk in private?' he said, putting an extra strong Beijing twang in his voice.

Li frowned. 'There's nothing you can't show Chao, here. Who are you?'

'My name is Bai Lifan,' Bao replied. 'I'm just a small businessman. But my cousin is a policeman. At a place called Huashan.' He took a package out from under his coat and unwrapped it. 'He got hold of this. He told me to bring it to you. He says you'll offer me a good price for it. Tang Dynasty, he says it is.'

Li betrayed no emotion in his face, but the way his hands caressed the plate showed that he knew its worth at once.

'My cousin says there's plenty more where that came from,' Bao went on.

'May we know the name of this cousin of yours?'

'No.'

Li glanced back down at the plate. 'You should tell me something so I can trust you. How did your cousin get hold of this?'

'Through the chief security officer, Wu. He caught Wu stealing it. Rather than turn Wu in, he made him tell his story and let him in on the act.'

'Should I speak to Wu to check that?'

Bao paused. How much should he reveal? 'My cousin says that unless you can speak to the dead, there would be no point.'

Li smiled.

'My cousin is eager to replace Wu as your supplier,' Bao went on.

'He reckons he can do that, does he?'

'Yes. I don't know the details. I don't want to. All I want is to do business.'

'I'll need time to look at this piece, of course.'

Bao gave a nod. 'I'll need some kind of deposit. A gesture of trust.'

'You don't trust me?'

'I don't trust anyone.'

'Shall I do him over, boss?' Chao put in.

Li paused. Then spoke. 'No, Mr Bai is wise to ask for a deposit. I'll give you five hundred yuan,' he told Bao. 'Meet me here again in two days.' The gangster held out a hand for him to shake. Bao breathed a sigh of relief.

'Wait here while I fetch the money,' said Li. 'Chao will keep you company.'

The boss went off. Chao began staring. 'Don't I know you from somewhere?'

Bao shook his head. 'I don't think so.'

'I'm sure I do.'

'This isn't really my usual business.'

'No. Bit of luck that, having a cousin in the police force.'

'Everyone needs some luck.'

Chao scowled, subjected Bao to further scrutiny, then seemed to lose interest. Li returned with the money and counted it out meticulously.

'Chao, show Mr Bai to the exit.'

The minder did as he was told.

*

Bao took a great deep breath – OK, so there was a little smog today from the factories around the capital, but any open air was better than the inside of that hotel – and began his walk back into town. At the bridge over the ring road, he paused, both to watch the traffic and to double-check that the man in the brown jacket was following him. Then he carried on.

The entrance hall of Dongcheng District Number Five Hotel was a narrow corridor perpetually blocked with luggage, customers, rubbish bins and deliveries for the kitchens. Today, two Western backpackers were sitting morosely on the one chair, hoping the receptionist would relent and give them a room. As they hadn't offered her any money, they were in for a long wait.

Bao pushed his way past and walked up the cold, stone stairs to the fourth floor. He collected his key from the floor attendant, paused to spit into the floor spittoon then let himself into Room 418. It smelt of mould, damp, disinfectant and stale cigarettes. Home from home for the likes of 'Bai Lifan'.

He sat down on the rock-hard mattress. It would take the man in the brown jacket a while to find out which room he was in.

Perfect, as Bao needed time to calm down after his meeting with Li and Chao. A little deep breathing, a browse through the war comic he had brought for Bai to read – it was all about Yunnan, 1979, and an attack on a Vietnamese-held ridge by a brave platoon commander. What he wanted most of all was a smoke, but bringing the Pandas had been a mistake. Finally, he took out his wallet and spread the money on the bed.

Though he knew it was coming, the rap on the door shocked him.

'Who is it?' he said cautiously.

'A friend of Luo Pang's.'

Bao scooped up the cash and bundled it under the pillow.

'I need to talk,' the voice continued.

'What about?'

'You ought to know. I'm not armed. And I've come alone.'

'How did you know I was here?'

'I followed you. Look, it's urgent. If you don't open up, you'll regret it.'

'In what way?'

'There's someone coming! Just let me in.'

Bao did so; the man in the brown jacket burst in and scuttled over to the bed. Only when the door was locked did the new arrival relax, pulling out a packet of Flying Horse cigarettes and offering one to Bao. Bao took it with apparent gratitude and lit up.

'What do you want?' said Bao.

The man lit up too, and seemed to enjoy having a carpenter's rasp shoved up and down his throat. 'To do business. Li will not offer you much for that plate.'

'What plate?'

'Chao told me.'

'Chao?'

'If you won't be straight with me, I'll go. I'm making you a good offer. Anything from Huashan, I want to do business with you. Pottery, statues, bronze, silver, gold ... I'll pay a decent price.'

'How decent?'

'I'll double any offer Li makes.'

'And supposing Li finds out? I've heard he isn't exactly keen on people who betray him.'

'That's my problem.'

'It could be a big one.'

'He's not that clever.'

'Isn't he? I've heard he's got contacts with some big brothers.'

The man looked at him. 'You've heard a lot.'

'Of course I fucking have. Do you think I'd just walk into that place without finding out as much as I can about it?'

'No ... What else do you know about Li?'

'Enough not to mess with him unless the alternative is a great deal of money.'

The man smiled.

Bao took another puff on the cheap cigarette. 'I don't want it being traced back to me or to my cousin. Li's organization seems to be cop-proof. How's yours?'

'Solid. And wealthy. Plenty of cash, just waiting to be spent.'

'Sounds good. How about some kind of payment in advance?'

The man looked shocked.

'It sounds reasonable to me,' Bao continued. 'If I'm to trust you ...'

'I'll – see what I can do.'

'Meet me in Beihai Park, tomorrow morning, ten o'clock. With one thousand yuan. Or else no deal.'

The man sucked on his Flying Horse. 'Tell me the name of your cousin.'

'You're joking!'

'I need security, too. If I'm going to cheat on Li … '

'I'll tell you in Beihai, once I've seen that money.'

'OK.' The man glanced at his watch. 'Make sure you're not followed there.'

'I'll make sure,' said Bao.

'You didn't even notice me.'

'I wasn't expecting to be followed. I'll be properly careful this time.'

'Do that.' The man chucked his cigarette on to the floor. 'Third bench along from the south-west gate.'

'I'll be there.'

*

The sentry saluted as Bao, back in uniform, entered HQ. But there was an odd look in the fellow's eye, one Bao had seen before, aimed at people in trouble. In his office, he found a note from Secretary Wei. *Contact me at once.*

'Bullying bastard,' said Bao, scrumpling it up, raising his arm to chuck it at the bin then stuffing it in his pocket.

He took out his notebook and read carefully through it. Then he began to write. He wrote down everything he could: Security Officer Wu's treachery and death, the falsity of Jasmine Ren's confession, the probable fate of her father, the *Yi Guan Dao* and their penetration of the Qianlong Hotel.

He was near the end of this, when his phone rang. He cursed – would this be a summons from Wei? – but it was someone wanting to speak to a Detective Superintendent Qiao. Bloody switchboard again.

He put the phone down angrily – then a new thought came into his mind.

He took out a sheet of paper and began drawing on it. Another one of his 'mind maps', but this time with the thefts at the centre. Radiating out from it, lines leading to anyone or anything connected with the thefts. Then lines between these connections. Possibilities. Stories.

This time there were no gaps.

Finally, he added a new section to his document. It said what he reckoned had happened to Xun Yaochang. Of course, he had no proof. Hopefully he soon would. Then put the document into an envelope, sealed it and addressed it to Chai. To be opened, at once, in case of death or serious accident.

*

'Bai Lifan' reached his rendezvous early, refreshed from a few hours' sleep back at the hotel. He found the bench, sat reading his comic – the heroic lieutenant died on the last page, praising the Motherland – then stared out at the lake in front of him. Mandarin ducks, two parks policemen in a rowing boat, seeds falling like snow from the weeping willows along the shore.

'Good morning!'

The man in the brown jacket was on time.

'Morning,' Bao replied. He glanced round to see if the man was alone. He was. 'You've got the money?'

The man took out a fat manila envelope and handed it over. Bao gave it a squeeze.

'Open it if you want.'

Bao did so. Ten little bundles of red ten-yuan notes. They even looked genuine.

'Now tell me the name of your cousin,' the man went on.

Bao paused, pretending to be searching for a last-minute get-out. 'His name is Bao,' he said finally. 'Bao Zheng. He's a mid-ranking inspector in the *Xing Zhen Ke*.'

What would the man do next? Beihai was a public place: Li's agent was hardly likely to take out a gun and shoot him. More likely, he would just smile, chat about business for a bit then report back to the Qianlong. Someone would come and liquidate Bai Lifan later. Possibly the same person whose job it would then be to liquidate Bao.

The Triad man nodded his head. 'Bao ... Zheng ... Obviously I've got to check there is such a man there – but I think we can trust each other from now on.'

'I'm sure we can.'

They agreed on a coded system of communication then parted, each glowing with the satisfaction of thinking they had fooled the other.

*

The slow train from Beijing pulled into Little River Station. Bao got out, stretched – the train had been crowded, but he wasn't in a position to ask for the use of an official car. A rosy-cheeked woman in an immaculate Chinese Railways uniform checked his ticket, then Bao walked out underneath the SERVE THE PEOPLE banner and stood in the forecourt of the rural station.

"Taxi?" called out a man on a motor-bike.

Bao shook his head. He wanted to finish his journey on foot.

It was not long before he was in the country and surrounded by country noises; wind hissing in young wheat, the chug of a water pump, the tinkle of water through a sluice. Men and women were working in the fields, the way his own family had for generations. Now, he had moved on. That's what you did in Nanping Village. Get out. Fight your way up the ladder ...

... And then, if you got the politics wrong, get kicked down again.

Another rural sound, an air horn. A shaky, rusting *Liberation* truck was lumbering up the road behind him. Bao's rib had begun to hurt, so he flagged the truck down. He showed his Police ID, and the driver beckoned him up into the cab.

'D'you investigate murders?' said the driver as the vehicle clanked into gear.

'Sometimes.'

'Any really big ones?'

'They're all about the same size.'

The driver went back to chewing his beetlenut with a loud sucking noise. Then he spoke again. 'D'you have anything to do with the Triads?'

Bao felt a shiver of fear. Surely not ... 'Sometimes,' he replied, trying to sound as offhand as possible.

The man grinned. 'I've heard that the Triads cut guys' dicks off and stuff them in their mouths. Is that true?'

'It has been known to happen, yes.'

'I've often wondered – do they do it after the victims are dead or before?'

'I'm not sure.'

A cyclist wobbled into view, and the truck driver blasted him off the road with his klaxon.

'In Italy, the Mafia stuff live rats up people's arses.'

'Really.'

'They don't feed them for a week beforehand – the rats, I mean. They're hungry.'

'I'm sure they are.'

'Real hungry.'

Clank. Another gear change.

'I'd like to be in the police. This job is boring. D'you get to shoot people? Like on Tiananmen Square? Bam! Bam! Fucking students. Troublemakers. Served 'em right ... '

Bao pointed to a farm entrance up ahead. 'This'll do fine,' he said. 'Thanks for the lift.'

*

It was about three kilometres to the Huashan turning then another four up to the camp. At the top of the climb, the ground levelled and the fir trees that filled the bottom part of the valley thinned out. Bao noticed an old foresters' hut set back from the track. He walked across to examine it. No, nobody had been here for ages. He returned to the track and emerged into the upper valley. Mount Huashan rose up in front of him: the path, the caves, the summit. The perfect place to fulfil his plan.

*

'Bao Zheng!' Team-leader Chen looked up from his scrawny duck and overcooked rice at the inspector, who had just entered the canteen. 'I didn't expect to see you here. I thought – '

'Didn't my message get to you?' Bao cut in.

'No.'

The inspector shook his head in pretend disapproval.

'Secretary Wei said you were to stay in Beijing,' Chen went on.

'Nobody told me. That new phone switchboard is dreadful.'

Chen looked just about to launch a defence of it, but even he couldn't manage it. '*Aiya!*' he said instead.

Bao chose to eat alone. Given his new political dubiousness, nobody would join him anyway. Alone he would be more noticed, too, which is what he needed. He gazed round at his fellow diners.

The security man Wu, the inspector was sure, had simply been part of something larger. He would have been great for getting stuff off the mountain, but up to Beijing? Someone else had to be involved. Another guard? Or someone senior? Bao had a strong feeling that the latter was the case, which had been strengthened by Li Dehong's reaction to his suggesting he replace the dead security man. The Triad had someone senior here … Who? He had an idea who, but that was still very much in the territory of *what is presumed*.

Professor Qiao and Dr Jian were sitting together for once, apparently discussing some academic topic. Qiao? Some Triads admitted women – one group of female blue lanterns had become notorious during the Boxer uprising – but he could not see this dignified, serious-minded lady joining up. So he had only had a brief, and very formal interview with her. Should he have asked for more?

Jian was much more obviously a mystery. How did he command all that influence back in Beijing? Through conventional *guanxi,* or because of his membership of a powerful, covert organization like the *Yi Guan Dao*?

Team-leader Hei Shou sat alone, too. What had happened at that factory?

Wu's former deputy, Fen, was a suspect, too. He was much sharper than his former boss. Too sharp for someone in such a junior position? Maybe.

And then there were Bao's own colleagues. Sergeant Fang, who had volunteered to stay at Huashan. Inspector Zhao: ambitious – had the lure of all that money been too much for him? Team-leader Chen, who had botched this investigation so thoroughly. With more than his usual incompetence?

Tomorrow, I will find out for sure, Bao told himself.

After dinner, most people went to the mess hut for a drink. Bao bought CSO Fen a Tsingtao, and requested official permission to climb to the top of the mountain. It was granted. Then he joined his colleagues, who reluctantly let him into their circle.

'I shall be making observations from the mountain-top tomorrow,' he said in a loud voice.

'Why?'

'Yes. I have this theory – there are eagles up there. I think that someone might have been training them to take stolen objects to a special place.'

Inspector Zhao's eyes widened. Chen began shaking his head. People from another table had put their drinks down and were listening.

'Does anyone have any better ideas?' Bao went on.

'I'm sure it wouldn't take me long to think of some,' Dr Jian muttered at another table.

'Eagles … ' said Chen. 'You're on your own with this one, Bao Zheng.'

'I know. That's fine.' Bao took out his wallet and produced several ten-yuan notes. 'Maotai, anyone? Dr Jian? Comrade Hei?'

When Bao said good night and headed back to his quarters, Team-leader Chen came with him.

'What the hell's this all about, Bao Zheng?'

'What?'

'This eagle rubbish.'

'It's an idea. I got it from one of the guards on Huashan. Listen to the People. Follow the Mass Line.'

'It's absurd.'

'You have better ideas, Lao Chen?'

Bao's boss winced. 'Take a day up there if you must.'

'It could work, Comrade Team-leader.'

'I suppose so.' Chen paused, as if he were about to say something else, then turned away. 'Good night.'

'Good night,' Bao replied, trying to keep the cheerfulness out of his voice.

*

The inspector packed what he needed for the next day's vigil, then crept out of his cabin. He had a story ready for the guard on the camp gate. He walked back to the tree-line and found the old foresters' hut. His pack made a pillow; the night was warm so he had no need of blankets. The insects were a nuisance, but much less of a threat than a Triad member with murder in mind.

Bao slept well.

He awoke at dawn – no alarm needed – to the sound of birds, got up and did some *taijiquan*. Early sunlight was slanting down through the trees, and the ancient martial exercises filled him with simple physical well-being. Man and nature united, the Daoist ideal. Then he set off back towards the mountain.

By seven o'clock he had reached the caves, surprising the night-shift with his early arrival. As he sat chatting over a mug of tea, he glanced idly through the registers to check who was already on the mountain. Nobody on his list of suspects.

He set off again. Out on the cliff-face it was beginning to get warm. He glanced down into the valley. Soon it would be filling with heat like a cauldron.

Chapter Seventeen

Bao Zheng scrambled up the last few yards of the ridge and lay down, panting with exhaustion, on the summit of Mount Huashan.

A glance at his watch, a sip of water, five minutes to recover his breath, then it was time to remind himself of the exact layout of his chosen fortress. He walked to the end of the gully and peered over the side. It was as he had remembered it, a sheer drop for hundreds of feet. He climbed the two ridges: no other way up here, either.

The Triad member has to act, he told himself, and act quickly. He or she will either want to negotiate or to kill me. Either way they'll have to show their hand.

He, Bao, needed the truth quickly, too. To save Jasmine Ren. To save himself, or at least his career. To solve the case, as he would be taken off it after the next Struggle Meeting. To do justice for Xun Yaochang, though some people would argue he didn't deserve it – the two cases were, of course, linked, something he should have understood more clearly earlier.

He tried a practice walk back up the gully covering an imaginary opponent with his Type 77 service revolver, then set to his final task. It took him about half an hour to build the dummy, a cairn of stones about three feet high across the entrance point where the ridge met the summit, with a jacket wrapped round it, his cap on the top and his binoculars balanced on a stone jutting out at the front. The final touch was a mask that Bao had bought in Dazhalan Alley, of Wu Sheng, a minor and thus plain-faced character from Beijing Opera.

He stood back and admired his handiwork. He needed to fluff the jacket arm out a bit more and raise the collar a fraction to hide the corner of the mask. How would 'he' look then, through field glasses or through a telescopic lens? Perfect.

He left his artwork, found some shade and settled down into it. He tried to relax – he would, after all, have advance warning as his quarry approached up the stony path. Then a scratching noise behind him made him wheel round and point a shaking gun at a small lizard ambling across the gully.

Relax!

He did a few *qigong* exercises to slow his heart-rate. Then he polished his gun, checked the ammo, glanced at his watch.

Ten a.m.

Be patient. Three feet of ice are not formed in one day.

He took out his notebook, and worked methodically through it.

He didn't like what it was telling him, but such was police work.

*

By half-past eleven, the sun was blazing in a cobalt sky. All the shade that had greeted him that morning had disappeared; the mountain-top seemed to glow with heat. The two waterbottles that Bao had lugged up the path now seemed inadequate, and he cursed himself for underestimating this factor. He might have to think or act fast, and dehydration would slow him down. Still, it was done now.

Another thing he hadn't thought through properly was the hoist, which from time to time clanked into action. Bao had imagined he'd always be able hear anyone approaching, but the noisy motor killed that chance. But again, he'd have to live with that.

*

Midday came and went. Only crazy people worked in this temperature – which, of course, made it a perfect time for someone to slip past the guards. The heat was blistering. Stay alert.

One o'clock.

Half past one.

Why was the prey not taking the bait? Had he miscalculated? Had he missed something that would later seem ridiculously obvious?

Then he heard it. A distant noise, hard to place, even recognize, but somehow unusual. Then something he did recognize, the clatter of a pebble.

Someone was coming. That someone had to be Wu's boss, the Triad's senior operative at the site of the thefts, the person who held the key to the whole business.

Bao could hear footsteps, now. He began to crawl towards the cairn. Then the footsteps stopped. Silence.

Bao stopped too. Then he heard the thwacking sound of a suppressed pistol and a bullet sang past him.

Thwack! A second shot shattered the Wu Sheng mask and sent the dummy's cap flying into the air.

Whoever had fired thought he had just spattered Bao Zheng's brains all over the top of Huashan.

Fine. They would then come up to the summit and either make the shooting look like suicide or just push the body off the back of the mountain. He would be ready for them.

Bao paused, till the footsteps started again. He clicked the catch off his pistol and wriggled the last metre to a small rock near the cairn, from which he could see the top part of the ridge.

The person climbing it came into view.

Bao let out a long sigh. He'd been right.

'Why?' he asked himself. This man was on the fast promotion track: just stay on it and he'd get to positions of seniority that he, Bao, could never dream of. He had considered this man a friend, too.

When Inspector Zhao was close enough, Bao levelled his revolver at him and called out, 'Put your gun down.'

Zhao nearly lost his footing with surprise – which was not what Bao wanted.

'The gun. Down. Or I'll just shoot you now.'

Zhao had his composure back almost at once. 'I wouldn't do that, Zheng. People down there will get the wrong impression.'

'Put the gun down. Now kick it over the edge. I mean it.'

'OK,' said Zhao.

Bao watched the weapon spiral out of view. He knew he should simply arrest Zhao now and get him down to base. But he was suddenly filled with curiosity.

'Now come up here,' he said.

When both men were facing each other on the mountain-top, he made Zhao take off his uniform and throw it over to him. With one hand, he searched through the clothes for weapons, while with the other he kept his pistol locked on his former colleague.

'I want the whole story. If I think you're lying, I'll kill you. Understand?'

Zhao nodded.

'Let's start with the murder.'

Zhao's surprise looked genuine. 'Wu fell off the mountain. You know that.'

'Of Xun Yaochang.'

'Ah ... Why ask me?'

'Because you are the killer.'

Zhao put on a puzzled face. Fake, Bao told himself.

'And your story there is ... ?' Zhao asked in a slightly mocking tone.

'I don't know the exact details. But I imagine it's something to do with that bloody switchboard at work. I think Xun called up wanting to speak to me, to tell me all he knew about the Triad and its activity. Revenge for Ren Hui's forbidding his daughter to see him. Or maybe he'd seen a Triad execution, and suddenly come to his senses about the organization he had signed up for. Or maybe the money helped – that's a nice reward for information leading to catching the thief, isn't it?

'Of course, it probably also helped when he realized he could meet me at the opera. I go there in uniform and some people know me. He probably asked around and found out who I was. Obviously he didn't ask the ticket seller I spoke to, but there are other people. Imagine his delight when he finds out I'm also working on a case involving one of his employer's activities! So he rings up. Am I going to be at the opera tonight? But thanks to the switchboard, he is put through to you, not me. So you say, 'Of course I'll be there' and arrange to meet him. A quick disguise – a cheap jacket and some shades – and off you go. How am I doing?'

Bao didn't need to ask, as his former colleague's expression was one of shock.

'Speculation,' Zhao said limply. 'Not a shred of proof for any of it.'

'That means it's true. I knew it was, but it's good to get confirmation. I assume you didn't think I'd actually be attending the event, too. No, I can see that's the case. That is what prompted you to take such a risky step. Your original plan must have been to take him off straight away for a meal and pump him for information. Once that was done, a couple of your *Yi Guan Dao* goons would turn up and either kill him on the spot or take him away to be disposed of in their chosen, and no doubt very unpleasant manner. But he must have said something like 'No, we're both opera lovers, let's see the performance first'. So in you went. Seats at the back, for an unobserved getaway if anything untoward happened. Then I appeared, and taking those seats turned out to have been a very wise precaution. Quick action – while it's noisy, you get the knife out and kill him. Where did you learn that trick? On some 'fast-track' promotion course?'

Zhao smiled. 'This is all about envy, is it?'

'It's about the truth, Zhao.'

'It's about a fantasy you've dreamt up because – '

'You've got a bloody cheek. You tried to murder me a few minutes ago. Now you're trying to bullshit me.'

Zhao fell silent.

Fine, thought Bao. Silence can be the interrogator's friend.

Finally, Zhao looked up at Bao with a new look of confidence on his face. 'OK,' he said. 'So what if I killed Xun whatever his name was? He was a gangster. You've seen men of twice his quality tortured and sent away to rot in labour camps and – '

'It's not like that any longer, and you know it.'

'Do I? I've got a little story to tell, too. It's about you.'

'I don't need to hear stories about myself. Tell me about CSO Wu. Not how he died, I know that. But about how you first teamed up with him. I assume you caught him stealing something, and, rather than turn him in, decided to join him. And I guess you set up the link with the *Yi Guan Dao*. Wu wasn't the brightest of men. He was probably just pilfering. Hiding stuff up in those upper caves, was he? You came in and made it all a proper operation. Nice idea about hiding the statues in the shit from the latrines … '

'That was his idea actually,' said Zhao combatively. 'He was cleverer than you think. He was also cleverer at hiding things than you think. As was I – some of the items aren't even in China any longer. So now there is only one person on the planet who knows where they all are. You're waving a gun at him. I don't think the authorities will be very pleased if you kill that person.'

Bao grimaced. He had heard enough. 'Inspector Zhao Heping, I am arresting you on the following charges. The murder of – '

'I haven't finished yet,' said Zhao. 'There are people I know who will be particularly displeased. Senior people, who prefer a different story. The story I just promised to tell about you. The one you were so keen not to hear. Perhaps you should let me tell it to you.'

Bao paused. Stop this now. Get his prisoner off the mountain. But he was curious. And maybe he did need to hear.

'OK,' said Bao. 'Tell me.'

'I'd like to roll the clock back a couple of years. Spring 1989. You and your student pals at the census office.'

'They weren't my pals.'

'You liked them, though, didn't you? You belonged with them, I think. You could have taken your little scroll with "Justice" written on it and shown it to them. You could have all sat around having a serious philosophical discussion about it – until your old pals, the Army, came and shot them all, of course.'

'That's got nothing to do with these robberies!'

'It's got everything to do with them. Why are we both sitting here on this mountain-top? Because of June 1989 and our reactions to it. Your feelings were obvious, Zheng. Your work went to pieces; you had to be parked behind a desk to keep you out of trouble. Your marriage fell apart. You said and did nothing, of course. I don't criticize you for that. The bird that sticks its head up is the one that gets shot.' Zhao held his fingers out like a pistol, aimed them at Bao and clicked the imaginary trigger. 'Of course, it's not very honourable what you did, pretending there was nothing the matter – '

'I don't have to listen to this from a murderer!'

'You have to listen to it from someone. For the last two years that someone has been you. Now it's me. Quite a relief, I'd imagine. Now, how d'you think I felt about Tiananmen?'

'Why should I care?'

'Because you have to know who's on your side?'

'I'm not on your side. The *Yi Guan Dao* are a bunch of gangsters and murderers.'

'Just like your beloved Army at Muxudi. What was it like, Zheng, the evening they opened fire? I've only read the internal Party documents; they're always so dry. How did it *feel* to be there, to see Chinese soldiers shooting unarmed Chinese civilians? They used Kalashnikovs, didn't they? A 7.62 calibre bullet with a muzzle velocity of six hundred metres a second, fired at close range. *Ai*, that must have been messy. Blood and bones and guts all over the place. Pretty young girls blown to bits by your beloved military. Those cubicle walls are pretty thin, Zheng, and I don't think it's Chen who shouts "They have no weapons!" in his sleep.'

Bao tried not to listen, but his ears had begun to ring with the screams of that crowd. He saw that girl pitch forward and the blood pump out of her back. He felt that rage rising within himself: helpless, treasonable, unspeakable. 'That's ... nothing to do with ... ' he mumbled.

Zhao ignored him. 'I was disgusted by Tiananmen, too. I wasn't there on the night, but I saw enough. There was a young man who stood in front of a line of tanks. They had to stop – there were Western cameramen about. But we got him in the end. I was in the station when they brought him in. He'd been beaten about a bit, but not as much as later on. Of course, in the end they took him out and shot him. A braver man than I'll ever be, forced to kneel down and die in the dust like a dog.

'That decided for me, actually. Get out. Tell the truth. I didn't know how; I didn't know when; I just decided. Wu gave me my chance.' Zhao paused. 'Of course, it could be your chance, too.'

'My chance?'

'To tell the world the truth.' Zhao smiled. 'Come with me. I've a million dollars' worth of stuff hidden away in Hong Kong. Nobody searched my luggage when I went out there. We could split it. Five hundred thousand dollars each. Look on it as a reward, for doing what you want to do and what you know deep down that you have to do: tell the truth.'

'Never!'

Zhao nodded. 'Ah. So you don't *really* care about Muxudi and those kids after all. That's nice to know. Underneath all the brave talk, when it really matters, you really are just another finger-puppet, jiggling around with the Party's finger up your arse. Just like Wei and Hong and all those other timeserving scumbags. I thought you might have more principles than them. Ah, well, I was wrong. You deserve what they're going to do to you.'

'Do?'

'There's another story going the rounds, Zheng. You're something to do with the thefts. Nobody's quite sure what – that's what I've come up here to find out. But so many things point that way. Look at your record!'

'I've just solved a murder!'

'A neat little diversion. They're looking to close down this operation here. A scapegoat would round things off perfectly. Someone with a record of hidden, suddenly exposed dissent, of political unreliability. Someone like ... well, you. Everything neatly tied up, the way the people in charge like it – the people who ordered the killings you saw at Muxudi. The people who killed that young student. The people you could go and tell the world about, but you haven't got the guts to so you'll let them destroy you instead.'

'That's not…' Bao began. But images were crowding in on him. The Struggle Session. The face of his accuser, Hong. Muxudi. That girl.

He suddenly felt sick. His hand on the gun began to quiver.

'You're the perfect scapegoat, Zheng. All set up and ready to destroy. Which the bigshots will do with as much compunction as you or I swatting an insect.' Zhao illustrated his point with a mime of flicking some creature off the back of his hand. 'Just another traitor unmasked and dealt with.' He grinned. 'And there's nothing you can do about it.'

Bao felt himself trembling. What did he believe? What was right?

He was startled by the noise. His own gun, going off unintended as his finger twitched on the trigger. The bullet slammed into the rock by Zhao's head. The sound echoed round the valley then died away, swallowed by its vastness.

Bao spoke slowly. 'Inspector Zhao Heping, I am arresting you on the following charges.'

'You're crazy, Bao Zheng. They're out to get you down there.'

'For fifty-six counts of theft from Huashan archaeological site – '

'This is the only chance you'll ever get!'

'For membership of an illegal organization –'

'Get out and tell the world the truth!'

'For the attempted murder of a police officer –'

*

Bao watched Zhao pick his way down the ridge then followed, gun in hand.

'You can still change your mind,' Zhao told him as he set off down the path.

'Keep walking.'

'Think about what I said. About Muxudi, about the money – '

'One more word, and I'll shoot.'

'Who's waiting down there for you? Secretary Wei – '

Bao fired – wide, but it had the desired effect. Zhao continued in silence: the only sounds were the two men's footsteps, the pounding of Bao's heart and the screeching of a nest of eaglets frightened by the shot.

Escape from bullies like Wei and liars like Hong. The freedom to speak his mind about Tiananmen Square. Half a million dollars. For a moment Bao saw Amy Lim in his imagination again. Not even that lovely nurse Miss Lin had Amy's effortless class, and with that kind of money he could find …

'Keep walking!' he told himself.

High in the sky, the mother eagle had heard the sound of her young and turned to investigate. She saw intruders. Filled with fury, she dived for the nearest one.

Bao didn't even have time to get a shot in. He had to throw up his hands to protect his face. An instant later, the eagle's claws tore into them. Bao heard the rattle of approaching footsteps.

The gun. He had to get the gun. He lowered a hand; the eagle's talons skinned his face right next to his eyes. His fingers found the Type 77 and jerked at the trigger. Boom! The bird gave a screech of fear and backed off. But now Zhao was upon him. A stone smashed into his forehead. For an unspeakable moment, Bao lost all sense of balance. He flung his hands out in a desperate grab to stop himself falling. The gun clattered away, but at least one hand found a crevice and locked on to it.

Zhao unleashed a punch that drove his stomach up into his ribs. A kick followed, aimed at his groin and only deflected by a flailing leg. A second punch, to Bao's still healing rib, doubled him up helpless with agony. A second kick slammed into the base of his spine. Then Zhao was grabbing him, turning him over, rolling his helpless body towards the precipice.

Use the enemy's strength against him.

Bao didn't consciously summon the words; they just came to him. With his last ounce of energy – the pain was so intolerable that if this failed, he would be happy to die – Bao resisted Zhao's pressure. Harder, harder he pushed back, until he felt his assailant redouble his efforts. At the moment of maximum resistance, Bao grabbed his opponent's wrists and hooked his knees under his stomach, turning his legs into a lever.

Now it was Zhao's turn to lose balance. His feet swung up from under him and his whole body began cartwheeling over his intended victim with all the momentum he had put into his attack. He tried a last desperate grab at Bao, to drag him down too, but found nothing but air and was suddenly spiralling into the enormous emptiness of the Huashan valley.

Bao watched his ex-colleague fall with a strange feeling of detachment. Impact produced a revolting thud. His assailant's body bounced into the air, rolled over and over down the scree slope, and finally came to rest against a boulder.

Still the veteran policeman felt nothing. Then he leant over the precipice and was sick.

Chapter Eighteen

'How long am I going to be here this time?' Bao asked.

'Those ribs broken again, possible lung damage, severe abdominal bruising, lacerations to face and neck,' said Miss Lin. 'A good while. Then a trip to Beidahe to recuperate afterwards, if the recommendation goes through.'

Bao grinned. People like him didn't usually get to visit China's top seaside resort.

'Now, let's get these dressings sorted out.'

The inspector lay back and let Miss Lin – or Rosina, as she told him she preferred to be called – get on with her work. (He still wasn't sure he totally approved of this fashion for western names, but if you had to choose one, Rosina sounded nice.) She had just finished, when Team-leader Chen strolled on to the ward.

'Visiting hours aren't till two o'clock,' said Rosina sharply.

'This is Party business.'

'The patient is not to be disturbed.'

'I'm a senior official!'

'I don't care who you are. This my ward.'

'It's all right,' Bao butted in. 'He's a friend.'

Rosina looked disappointed, but let Chen stay. He came and sat by the bed.

'I hope they're looking after you all right,' he said in his official voice. 'You deserve the best.'

Bao shook his head. 'I was only doing my job.'

'Honourable sentiments, Comrade. Ones I shall pass on to our colleagues at the next Political Study Meeting.'

Bao winced at the words. In the last few days, he had relived his argument with Zhao over and over and over again. The thoughts it had inspired stung him deeper than his worst wounds. Several times he had tried to get out of bed and to run to the open, third-storey window and had had to be restrained – the last time by Sister Lin. Her gentle touch had done something the rough grip of the ward orderly had failed to do – embarrassed him into quietly going back to bed.

In that new frame of mind, he had been able to be more objective about the story Zhao had told him up there on the mountain. That bit about the man and the tanks – he'd asked Chai to find out about him, and nobody knew what had happened to that individual. Zhao's 'senior' contacts? Maybe true. But they would be smart enough to stay quiet, given the evidence. The idea that Zhao's catching Wu had turned him into a traitor was at best a half-truth – he must have been flirting with the *Yi Guan Dao* before, otherwise how could he have set up the network? And all that stuff about his having smuggled artefacts to Hong Kong. The whole business about the South had no doubt been some kind of diversionary tactic after Wu's death, but the idea that Zhao could have carried a whole lot of valuable artefacts to Hong Kong was ridiculous! The corrupt cop had lured him into a web of lies, part-planned, part-improvised.

And he, Bao Zheng, had nearly fallen for it.

'I'm afraid our raid at the Qianlong wasn't very successful,' Chen went on.

Bao winced.

'The people you told us about – Li, Chao, the other fellow – had all gone. On a flight to Taiwan, we subsequently discovered. And Li's office was empty: no papers, no antiques. When Zhao was killed, they must have realized the game was up.'

'You let them get away!'

'I know, we could have acted quicker. But there were, er, political aspects. Remember at the time you were under suspicion of counter-revolutionary sentiments. Not that I ever believed that for a moment, but it takes time to sort these things out.' Chen paused. 'You wait till you get a team of your own, Bao Zheng. You don't have nearly as much control over things as other people think.'

'If people like Wei and Yue have their way, that will never happen.' Bao sank back on to his pillows. He stared into space, then asked weakly: 'Any sign of Ren Hui?'

'No. We're doing our best. Does it really matter?'

'The truth always matters. I assume he was got rid of because he had become a security risk. What about Ren Yujiao? She's been released, I take it?'

'There are complications.'

Bao shook his head. 'Get her out now, Chen. Please. Use your influence, you're good at that. She's had enough.'

'It might be difficult,' said Chen.

Bao knew that meant 'no'.

*

A couple of days later, he told Rosina all about this. They often had long conversations, so long that some of the younger nurses had started making comments.

'You are really concerned about her, aren't you?' she said.

'Yes. It's wrong!'

'You must get her out then. You won't be happy otherwise. You'll be sitting on that beach, in all that luxury, hating every minute of it.' She smiled at him admiringly.

'Would you like to come with me?' he asked suddenly.

'I don't think that would be possible,' she said, lapsing back to official coldness at once.

Bao cursed himself for his ineptness. If he found himself another partner, he should get a shit-shoveller like himself, who talked in an accent everyone laughed at. They could sit around moaning about city folk and how stuck-up they all were and congratulate themselves on being morally superior.

Oh, well, at least nobody else had overheard the conversation. And the shame that now filled him would kill off any growing feelings for this woman, which otherwise he would have lugged around for ages.

'But I do like restaurants,' Rosina added, smiling again. 'And films. I'm very fond of films.'

*

Commissioner Da was in his office when Bao walked in. 'Bao Zheng! Nice to see you fit again!'

Bao sat down without being asked: the climb up the stairs had been painful. 'Thank you, sir.'

'You'll join me in some tea? I got hold of some best *tieguanyin* the other day.'

Bao smiled at the irony. Guanyin, the prize heist from Huashan, also gave her name to one of China's premier teas. Da began to spoon wizened black leaves out of a tin.

'I've come to see you about Ren Yujiao, sir,' said Bao. 'The young woman falsely accused in the Xun Yaochang case.'

The old man nodded. 'Chen mentioned her the other day. But there are problems. She faces charges of deception, perjury, wasting police time – '

'She was trying to protect her father's life, sir.'

'He was a gangster.'

'To us, yes. To her … '

The commissioner turned round. 'A policeman, like a soldier, cannot be sentimental. Our job is to enforce law.'

'Our job is to enforce justice, sir. Ren Yujiao was put in an intolerable position.'

Da was smiling. 'I like you, Bao Zheng. You believe in the sort of things we believed in at Yan'an. Not too many people around nowadays do. I'll see what I can do for this woman. Now, about your application.'

'Application? For the week in Beidahe?'

'No, to rejoin the Party. I gather there's some kind of delay.'

'Yes, sir.'

'There shouldn't be. I've arranged to handle the application myself. Wei can't judge character. He always takes black mares for yellow stallions – typical of a man who's spent his life behind a desk. I judge people by their actions. If you fill in this form here, I'll make sure you're reinstated to full membership by the time you get back.'

The old man held out a piece of paper. Bao took it, stared down at it, then spoke.

'That's kind of you, sir … '

'No need for that. The Party needs you.'

'But I want a little more time. To consider.'

'Consider? There's nothing to consider. If I say you're in, you're in.'

Bao paused. 'I'm not sure I want to be in, sir.'

Silence fell.

Da broke it. 'Don't want to?'

'I've been – thinking.'

'Too much thinking can be bad for you. You don't know what China was like in the old days. You've just read books. I've seen starving families, streets in Shanghai full of prostitutes – Chinese women selling themselves to foreigners to pay for opium imported by the British. The Party changed all that. It made us stand up. It gave us pride. And it still does.'

'Still?' Bao didn't mean to put it that bluntly; it had slipped out.

Da said nothing. His face was expressionless. Bao suddenly wondered again quite how well he knew this man. Outside, a siren wailed.

'I am aware of your misgivings about June 1989,' the veteran said after a long pause. 'I do not share them, of course. What happened was regrettable but necessary to prevent our nation sliding into anarchy. But that's not the point. The point is that your personal feelings do not give you the right to desert your public duty. Do you love your country?'

'Of course, sir.'

'Good. In the old days, there was a stock reply to that – then you must love the Party, too. But I know that in both our lifetimes, the Party has made mistakes. I spent some time in the countryside during the so-called Great Leap Forward, and saw starvation as bad as the old days. I suffered in the Cultural Revolution. Several of my colleagues did not survive those years. Do you think I have no bitterness, no anger about those things?'

'No, sir,' Bao said slowly.

'You're a young man, Bao Zheng. If you want to change things, you have time. But you won't change anything outside the Party. All you'll do is knock things down, destroy, snipe, disrupt. Get back inside and you can make real progress. I happen to believe that's the way things should be. You should serve your country first, change it second. Other people disagree – but the facts are indisputable. Outside the Party, you will have no influence, so your views and values will count for nothing.'

Bao tried to look calm, despite the war going on in his head.

'I'll make it easy for you,' the old man continued. 'One of Minister Hu's senior aides is the daughter of an old friend of mine. If I get your form on my desk by tomorrow, properly filled in, I'll phone her and tell her to get the Ren woman freed. It might take a few days – she's not *that* powerful – but it will happen.' Da paused. 'If I don't get that form back, then I'm afraid you will be campaigning on your own, for Ren Yujiao and for yourself. I know Wei and that little shit Hong are after your blood. I dislike them almost as much as you do – but if you won't serve your country any longer, then I can't keep them off you.'

He began rummaging a drawer. 'I also have this,' he said, producing a piece of paper. Bao recognized it at once as the memorandum he had sent about the students back in late May 1989, recommending patience and discretion.

'I rescued this before other, less friendly eyes saw it. I won't blackmail you with it; you have served your country too well. It will never leave this room while I can prevent that happening – but I'm not immortal. This will make a nice extra incentive for you. Rejoin the Party, and we can set fire to it next time you're up here.'

*

Bao looked up at his photographs. Lieutenants Bao, Wan and Yi, grinning at a Seagull camera.

He thought of Da: 'You won't change anything outside the Party'. The memorandum.

Jasmine Ren. 'Can I trust you?'

And now, Rosina. It was just a 'date' he had lined up with her – how strange that concept sounded at his age. And no doubt other men were keen to take her out. She might turn out to have all kinds of character defects – there had to be some reason why she was still unattached at her age. But maybe not. She certainly wouldn't be very impressed if he let Jasmine rot in prison because of his own scruples. She might prefer a Party member as a partner, too.

Bao felt annoyed with himself for letting such self-interest cloud his decision on this matter of public honour. Then he wondered how many other Chinese officials, not just in this era but over millennia, had faced the same dilemma of public duty versus private doubts. No doubt they all had their different sets of motives and problems.

He began to fill in his application.

*

Eddie Zhang met his two special guests at the bottom of the

drive.

'I've reserved the best seats in the house!' he told them. 'It's the least I could do after what you did for Jasmine, Inspector,' he went on. 'She told me all about it when she came to say goodbye.'

'Goodbye?' said Bao.

Eddie's face fell. 'She's gone abroad.'

'I thought you said she wasn't the type to desert her homeland.'

'It unbalanced her, this business with her father.' Eddie gave a shrug of resignation. 'She can start again in Taiwan. With her talent, she'll go far.'

'Taiwan?'

To join her cronies in the gang?

No. Bao was sure of that.

To seek revenge?

Possibly.

Maybe just to get on with her life.

He wished her that.

They began to walk towards the hotel.

'Er, you haven't introduced me to your lady friend,' said Eddie.

'Oh, sorry, this is Lin Xiangyu. Though I guess you'll prefer to call her Rosina.'

Eddie shook her hand and gave a foolish grin, his usual reaction to an attractive woman. They walked a little further.

'That looks impressive,' said Rosina, pointing at the site of the new pool.

Another grin from Eddie. 'Yes. It's going to be Olympic-size. I can get you tickets if you like.' He flushed with pride. 'D'you know, a month ago that was just a patch of lawn! Then they dug this huge hole, then poured in tons of concrete – '

'Concrete?' Bao cut in. 'When was that?'

'About three weeks ago. Maybe two.'

'Concrete,' Bao repeated thoughtfully.

'We've got a gala opening in a fortnight,' Eddie went on. 'You must be my guests!'

'Thank you,' said Bao. 'You'll come, won't you, Rosina?'

The woman said she'd be delighted.

Bao, now fully restored to his rank and Party membership, could order the pool dug up, but the Tourism Ministry would create havoc. And it was only a hunch. Ren Hui's body could have been disposed of anywhere. And even if it were there, the people who had ordered his killing were in another country with which there was no diplomacy, let alone extradition.

They reached the hotel entrance. The doorman bowed obsequiously; the lift took them up to the twentieth floor. TONIGHT IN THE STARLIGHT SUITE! TRADITIONAL CHINESE SILK AND BAMBOO MUSIC.

Eddie showed the guests to a front table. Polite applause from the small but select audience greeted the two performers, both men in their fifties, one with a reed flute, the other with a *qin*, a seven-stringed dulcimer that hadn't changed in two and a half thousand years since Confucius had mastered it. They gave long introductory spiel in Chinese and broken English, then began to play.

Bao, who had felt a little out of place as a guest in this western finery, suddenly felt totally at home.

*

'How did you like it?' he asked Rosina at the end.

She smiled. 'It was … different. Next time, though, let's do something more modern. There's a new Liu Guoquan movie. Did you see *Girl of the Times*?'

He shook his head. 'I don't go to the cinema much. So it will be a particular treat,' he added, suddenly thinking he was sounding negative.

Eddie had also organized a car to take them home, first Rosina to hers, then Bao back to Tiantan. On the last part of the ride, he recalled her parting smile and felt a great happiness.

Then, naturally, his thoughts went back to the mountain. Where were those artefacts? Hidden up there? If so, they would probably never be found. That seemed right, too. It was where they belonged. Old Professor Qiao, he reckoned, had felt the same.

Or had Zhao spirited some away, after all? Well, they were gone. Who knew where?

*

Cantopop echoed round the walls of the Golden Lotus Club in Wanchai. The young Englishman who had come in an hour ago was now sitting in the corner, telling Lily Wong about reinsurance and how important it was to the world economy. They finished their bottle – the club was almost out of '66 – then Lily set off across the dance floor. The youngster followed her, eager and nervous. His first night with a hooker! They went upstairs; Lily opened the door of her little room; the Englishman stood hesitantly on the threshold then followed her in.

'Nice room,' he said, grinning idiotically.

Lily smiled back. Plenty of time.

'What's the picture?' the youngster continued, pointing up at the mantelpiece.

Lily kept smiling. 'It's an ancient Chinese goddess. Guanyin. She looks after the poor, the weak, the sick.'

The young man grinned. He'd been brought up to regard these concerns as unimportant compared to the callings of God, Queen, country, money and social position. Especially the last two.

Lily began to undress him. As she did so, her mind went back to the real Guanyin she had back at home, the one that her Comrade from Beijing had given her, along with the plates, the brasswork and the parchments with ancient characters on. He'd promised her he'd be back to collect them, but he had never appeared. All he'd sent her was some kind of sketch with clusters of figures and strange, snaking diagrams on it. And two characters, *Fa Saan.* Flower Mountain: was that a place? She'd never heard of it. Still, she'd keep it safe. It might be worth something one day.

If he didn't come soon, she would sell the things he'd given her. Except Guanyin. If they turned out to be valuable, she could give up this life. Buy a bar herself, maybe – but not in Hong Kong, not with the Communists coming.

*

Printed in Great Britain
by Amazon